PRAISE FOR *THE ROAD TO WINTER*

'It's easy to see why Mark Smith's dystopian thriller has been compared with John Marsden's *Tomorrow When the War Began*. I barely came up for breath as the pages flew. So strap yourself in for a high-action ride.' *Kids Book Review*

'Assured, gripping and leaves you wanting more.' *Sydney Morning Herald*

'A riveting story of survival that questions the prices of freedom and safety as well as the value of an individual life...A breakout new series full of romance, danger, and a surprisingly engaging world.' *Kirkus*

'Finn's strong voice carries the story and leaves you wanting to know what will happen next.' *Books+Publishing*

'This post-apocalyptic tale has heroes and villains, humour and heartache, and plenty of excitement...A brilliant debut from an author to watch.' *BookMooch*

'Whenever I put the book down, I felt as if I'd been holding my breath...The world Smith creates is convincing, perhaps because he takes real-world scenarios and kicks them up a notch.' *New Zealand Listener*

'In the footsteps of John Marsden and Claire Zorn comes Mark Smith's first post-apocalyptic novel—with two more to follow. Unforgettable.' Best Books for Kids 2016, *NZ Listener*

'A beautiful and intimate story...Like the best YA fiction, *The Road to Winter* is sure to appeal just as much to an adult audience.' *Otago Daily Times*

'One of those novels that once you start reading, it is nearly impossible to put down again...An unforgettable novel about survival, honour, friendship and love.' *South Coast Register*

'Thought-provoking...insightful and heartbreaking.' *Reading Time*

Mark Smith lives on Victoria's Surf Coast with his family. His first book, *The Road to Winter*, was published in 2016. *Wilder Country* is his second novel.

WILDER COUNTRY

MARK SMITH

t

TEXT PUBLISHING MELBOURNE AUSTRALIA

textpublishing.com.au

The Text Publishing Company
Swann House
22 William Street
Melbourne Victoria 3000
Australia

First published in Australia by The Text Publishing Company, 2017.

Cover and text design by Imogen Stubbs.
Cover photograph by Helen Rushbrook/Stocksy.
Typeset by J&M Typesetters.

Printed in Australia by Griffin Press, an Accredited ISO AS/NZS 14001:2004 Environmental Management System Printer

National Library of Australia Cataloguing-in-Publication
Creator: Smith, Mark, author.
Title: Wilder country / by Mark Smith.
ISBN: 9781925498530 (paperback)
ISBN: 9781925410778 (ebook)

For those we lost along the way:
Tom, Leonie and Adam

1

The morning air is cold but the storm from last night has cleared and the wind is feathering the peak at the river mouth. Rowdy waits patiently on the lookout platform while I change into my wetsuit and pull my board out from its hiding place in the tea trees.

Before long, I'm duck-diving under the waves as they hit the inside bar, the freezing water finding the holes in the stitching and my bare skin underneath. When I reach clear water, I catch my breath and ease into a steady rhythm, paddling towards the peak. The winter storms have shifted the sand and it'll take me a while to get used to how the wave is breaking. When I get close, I sit up on my board and take stock. The peak is further along the beach than I've seen it before, almost in line with the platform, but provided the channel is still shallow enough, the wave should break all the way through to the river mouth.

Sitting out here, it's hard not to remember what it was like before the virus: surfing with my mates, the beach dotted with swimmers and walkers, the lifesavers' flags flapping yellow and red in the offshore breeze. On the other side of the dunes the car park would be overflowing on a day like this, the road choked with cars and caravans and the town buzzing with holidaymakers. Across the river and up the hill, Mum would be out in the garden, weeding or pruning, and Dad would be in the shed stripping back an old table, the smell of dust and linseed oil hanging in the air.

But when I look now, I can see all the way back up the river to the road bridge and the ruins on the main street, the shells of burnt-out shops and abandoned cars. It's hard to keep track of time when you're on your own but there've been three winters since the virus spread beyond the cities, reaching us and forcing the town into quarantine. That's when Dad died. And two winters ago, I lost Mum. Everyone else in town was either killed by the virus or took their chances heading north, leaving me and Rowdy to fend for ourselves.

We did okay, hunting and fishing and staying out of sight. Then Rose came.

Everything changed the day she appeared on the beach, scared, injured and pregnant, an escaped Siley on the run from Ramage and the Wilders. Taking her in and hiding her unleashed a shit storm. First there was the journey north to find her sister, Kas, then the escape back to the coast with Willow in tow, and finally, on the worst night of my life, Rose dying as Hope was born.

The swell is a little unsettled and I need to be careful not to get too far inside the peak. Dad always said the best way of starting a surf was to take off on the biggest wave you could get. Opening your account, he called it. So I ease over the top of the first four waves, each one breaking a little further out, until I'm in perfect position for the next one. I barely have to paddle into the take off, just a couple of deep strokes and the rest is muscle memory. I'm a little slow to my feet, but I balance myself and feel the beautiful rush of the drop down the face.

As usual, I lose all sense of time in the water and before I realise it the sun's above the ridge and there are new storm heads building in the west. Kas and Willow will be awake and wondering when I'll be back. So I take one last wave, riding it all the way to the beach, where Rowdy paces up and down the sand, chasing seagulls he'll never catch. He brushes past my leg as we make our way back up the dune to the platform.

The winter has almost passed and Kas, Willow and I have welcomed the return of some warmth to the air. It's been a winter of storms, with huge fronts coming straight up from the south, smashing into the coast. There's damage all over Angowrie—big trees uprooted, roofs blown off and the river flooding right up into town on the king tides.

In a strange way the harsh weather's kept us safe. We've been isolated for months; the road north is blocked and there's snow on the ridges. As long as I've been alive it hasn't snowed this close to the coast, but the weather's so cocked up now, everything feels like it's never happened before. We figure the Wilders were forced back to Longley to sit out the winter, but with the warmer days, they'll be out on the hunt again soon.

It's been a tough time for all three of us, but Kas has been the worst affected. Rose's death hangs over everything she does. She stays in her room for days at a time, refusing food and snapping at Willow and me when we try to cheer her up. She's a different person now. I'd hoped when we got back to Angowrie she'd gradually work her way through her grief. But every time I've tried to comfort her, to hold her or even touch her, I've felt her resistance. No matter what we talk about, she always ends up back at Ray's place that night, Rose dying, Ramage arriving to claim his child and us running from the Wilders. She hardly mentions Hope—it's too hard, on top of all her grief, to think what might have happened to the baby.

I've spent the winter worrying about Ray. He's used to being on his own but he's so isolated out there in the Addiscot Valley. It's only a couple of hours away on foot but he's too old to travel far and I know the storms will have tested him. He'll be struggling to get out and work his garden, not that much would've grown in the cold months. Before the weather got really bad, I thought if we went out to visit him Kas could at least see where Rose was buried, but she kept putting it off, always finding excuses.

4

The first few weeks after Rose died were the hardest. The full force of winter hadn't arrived yet and we had to be extra cautious moving around Angowrie, not knowing if the Wilders stayed south of the main range. I didn't believe they'd leave us alone. They'd figure we had food supplies hidden somewhere and Ramage still wanted to take Kas back to Longley. As far as he was concerned, she was a Siley and his property.

Back then, I wasn't prepared to risk trapping along the fences. It's what they'd be expecting, that we'd return to a place we knew we could get food. As long as we stayed in town, kept out of sight, lit a fire only on moonless nights and got by as best we could, I thought we'd be safe. So we relied on what food we could pick off the reef, mostly pippies and mussels exposed at low tide.

Rowdy rushes ahead once we get close to home. By the time I'm through the back door he's lapping water from his bowl in the corner. Kas and Willow sit at the kitchen table peeling hard-boiled eggs.

Willow looks up and smiles. 'How was the surf?'

I cup my cold hands on the side of her face and she reels away. 'A bit chilly,' I say.

Kas forces a smile then goes back to the eggs. This is what she's like now, only half with us, hardly joining in, as though it would be some sort of crime.

With Kas off in her own world, Willow's become my shadow. She's always watching me, asking a million questions about rabbits and hunting and living off the land.

I decided last night that we should start trapping again and she's excited to get going.

After breakfast she sits on the back porch watching me oil the traps. The wind has turned and another storm is threatening. She pulls her favourite woollen coat tight around her shoulders. We needed to find some clothes for her when we got back from Ray's, so I went through all the houses in the area. Eventually, I found a heap of kids' clothes in a place at the top of Parker Street. She had a great time trying them on, parading up and down the hallway. Even Kas managed a smile.

'Show me how to do that,' she says, coming and kneeling next to me on the grass.

I work the trap's jaws open and shut while she drips oil into the spring. I look up and see the concentration on her face, everything focused on what she's doing, as though this is a skill she'll need to hang onto.

She pushes the hair off her face with an oily hand and catches me looking.

'What?' she says.

'Nothing,' I say, trying not to smile. She's easy to be around. I never have to second guess her or worry about upsetting her. She's turned out to be a tough kid.

The storm is short and sharp, exhausting itself in fifteen minutes. When we're ready to leave, I stick my head in the door and tell Kas we're heading up to the fences. She's still at the table with the same blank look on her face she's had since we got back from Ray's. I so much want the old Kas back, the one that was funny and warm. She looks the same, her hair thick and tangled and falling across her face, deep brown eyes, the skin dark around the birthmark on her cheek, but there's something missing—the spark that made her who she was. Even though she's been right here, sleeping in the next room, eating at the same table, warming herself by the same fire, she might as well be on another planet.

'I'm taking Wils with me,' I say.

'Sure. Whistle when you come back.'

This is the way she talks now, in short little sentences, like anything else is too much effort.

We head out with the traps, keeping to the back tracks and staying alert for any sign of danger. The storm damage is everywhere. Fallen branches and uprooted trees block our way at every turn. Only Rowdy is unconcerned, darting ahead, happy to be active again after a slow couple of months. He senses the familiarity of it, though this time with Wils included in our little party. It's easy to forget she's only nine or ten years old. She doesn't wander or dawdle like a kid anymore, she walks with purpose, keeping her eyes and ears open.

And she's been practising with the bow and arrows. At the beginning of winter she set up a target in the backyard, an old mattress with a bullseye painted in the middle. At the start, I think she did herself more damage than the target—she had big red welts on her arm where the string hit her—but gradually she got the hang of it. Now she can hit the target from the other side of the yard, and when she isn't practising, she'll be in the shed sharpening the metal tips of the arrows.

It takes twice as long to get up to the ridge as it would have before the winter. We approach the fence slowly but everything looks the same. The burnt-out hayshed is still a tangle of steel girders and blackened rafters, all collapsed into a heap. I know this place well—I've been setting my traps up here since before Mum died.

Further along we come to the gateway where I knocked Ramage off his trail bike. I'd strung a length of wire across the opening so he'd hit it at speed. He was injured and I had a knife at his throat, but somehow I couldn't finish him off. Now I wonder how things might have been different if I'd killed him when I had the chance. Maybe he wouldn't have attacked the valley, forcing us to escape with Willow. Maybe Rose would be alive. Maybe she and Hope would be living with us and Kas would be a different person.

Finding a small gap in the bottom of the fence, I dig the first trap in and push hard on the spring to set the plate. Willow squats next to me and watches.

'This is where you've gotta be careful, Wils. If the plate doesn't catch, it'll snap shut and you'll lose a finger.'

The plate holds and I sprinkle some dry leaves over the top to hide the metal. Willow is holding her breath. Rowdy knows to stay well clear. We set four traps at intervals along the fence.

It's slow going on the way back down. Willow walks out in front, checking every now and again to check I'm keeping up. When we reach the lookout above the old football ground we sit down for a rest and scan the town below for any sign of danger. From up here I can pick every street, every short cut and trail through the dunes. This is my town, my fortress against the Wilders. If they come again, I can outwit them; I know the terrain so much better than they ever will.

Willow sits next to me and says, 'When is Kas going to be happy again, Finn?'

'It's going to take a while, I think.'

Willow sighs and looks to the blue line of the horizon. 'She cries in the night,' she says.

'She'll get better. We've just gotta look after her until she does.'

'Finn!' Willow says suddenly. She points to where the main road winds down into town. There's movement, something catching the light. I can't hear anything above the sound of the wind whipping through the trees, but I watch a gap in the bush a little further down and wait to see what emerges.

There are maybe six or seven of them—we're too far away to work out who they might be, but they're moving slowly. I can't see any weapons but they're pushing handcarts piled with sacks. I'm hoping they're Drifters, like the ones that passed us when Harry had me blindfolded up above Pinchgut Junction.

Rowdy's picked up their scent and he stands to attention. Keeping low, we take off down the track to the river bridge, arriving before they get there. We make our way across and hide just off the road in a low stand of tea tree.

The first thing I want to see is that they're not Wilders. After a few minutes they come to the bridge and stop. There are six men and two boys, Drifters for sure. Their clothes hang off them and they hold rags over their mouths as though the air is dirty. Their hair is long and matted and their eyes dart left and right. One of them, a tall man with a stooped back, walks out onto the bridge and looks up and down the river.

Willow lies next to me holding her breath. Rowdy crouches low, ready to spring at them if he has to. I touch him gently on the nose but he stays alert. These are the first Drifters I've seen in Angowrie, the first to take their chances on passing through a quarantined area—at least I hope they're passing through.

The tall guy motions the others across. They stay in single file keeping their heads down and their mouths covered. As they pass us, I see how thin they are. Their eyes are dark and sunken, their arms and legs like sticks. I can smell them too—a stench of sweat and piss. Some are barefoot but a couple wear shoes that clomp on the asphalt road. The smallest two boys, about seven or eight years old, are at the back, struggling to keep up.

They continue along the road parallel to the river, the axles of their carts squeaking under the weight of their loads. We track them as they pass below the platform and make their way up the hill and out along the coast road.

I'm happy to see the back of them. Mum and Dad always said we should help people less fortunate than us, but all the old rules fell away after the virus. We probably could've given them some food, though we hardly have enough for ourselves, but who's to say they wouldn't have killed us for it. I stopped trusting people a long time ago. I don't feel good about it, but it's necessary now.

In the next couple of weeks we survive the last of the storms, hunkered down, hoping our little house will stand up to the weather. The appearance of the Drifters is a reminder that the spring will bring more danger. We've got no way of knowing what's happening outside Angowrie in the bigger towns like Wentworth, where I used to go to school, or further north in the larger cities, but people are moving again. Add to that the threat of the Wilders and things are going to change. Quickly, it seems.

We see out the winter, scrounging for food and huddling together to keep warm. I can't help but think back to my previous two winters, when there was just Rowdy and me doing the same, scrounging for food and huddling together for warmth. But everything has changed since Rose appeared on the beach.

More than ever, now, I need to find a way through to Kas, to open her up again. And not just because I want to feel her close to me. If we're going to make it through the summer, with the Wilders returning to settle old scores, all three of us will have to have to work together. It's the only way I can see us surviving.

2

Spring has taken ages to get here, but finally the storms have eased off and the few remaining fruit trees around town have started to blossom.

Today it feels like we've turned some sort of corner. The sun has got a bit of punch to it and we can feel it warming our winter bones. Willow wants to come down to the beach and watch me surf. Kas sits on the porch, stretching and flexing like a cat that's just woken up. She ties her hair back and turns her face to the sun.

'Me and Wils are going to beach,' I say. 'Wanna come?'

She's hardly been outside for months. The fresh air and

sunshine would do her good.

'I might come over later,' she says, but I can't tell whether she means it or not.

I've almost given up trying to convince her to do anything. Willow hasn't said as much but I reckon she feels the same way. She spends all her time with me and hardly bothers to tell Kas what she's doing. And Rowdy has adopted Willow—they go everywhere together.

As we make our way up to the platform, it's good to feel the sand under my feet and the northerly at our backs. The swell is dead straight, not too big, which is good because I'm a bit rusty. Willow and Rowdy race down onto the open beach. I change into my wetsuit, stash my clothes under the platform and follow them. The sets are lining up nicely but I want to make sure Willow understands we have to be careful, even though it's a beautiful beach day.

'Wils, we need a way of signalling each other in case there's any trouble,' I say.

'Like how?'

'If you want me to come in, hold both your arms up in the air and keep them there. I'll watch for you and if I see you signalling, I'll come straight in, okay?'

'Like this?' She stands on her toes and holds her arms up straight.

'Perfect. You'd make a great surf lifesaver.'

'What's that?'

'Never mind. Stay with Rowdy.'

The current is strong and by the time I make it across the bar, my arms are starting to feel it. It's good to duck dive under a set on the way out, keeping my eyes open underwater and watching the rolling force of the wave come at me. I sit up and look back at Willow, who's racing up and down the beach with Rowdy. Like every other time I've surfed over the past three years, I check up the river as far as I can see, then turn and paddle towards the peak. The water hasn't settled after the rain and there are little bits of weed and leaves that have been washed down the river. But the offshore wind is glassing off the surface and the waves are hitting the bar and peeling along the line.

What I've missed through not surfing much over the winter is doing something that's not just about survival for a change. But, for some reason, I feel uncomfortable today. I keep looking at the beach, where Willow has stopped running along the sand and is staring out to sea. I take a wave and paddle back out. When I look again, Willow has both her arms in the air. Kas is standing a little way behind her, arms in the air, too. My heart starts to race and I scan the dunes for signs of trouble before catching the next wave and belly-boarding in over the bar. I tuck the board under my arm and run towards them.

I'm out of breath by the time I get close enough to yell to them. 'What is it? Where are they?'

'Come here,' Willow calls.

I splash through the shallows until I reach her.

'What's going on?'

'I wanted you to come in,' Willow says.

The offshore blows her hair from behind, making it fly around her face like a halo. She puts her hands on her hips and juts her jaw out. 'I want to swim, Finn. I want to go in the water,' she says.

I'm relieved but a bit confused too. I look to Kas, who's standing a few metres back but she doesn't meet my gaze. 'What's stopping you?' I ask Willow.

'Come with me,' she says.

'Why?'

'We've never been in the sea before,' Kas says. 'Remember?' Her voice sounds different, more lively, and there's a half smile on her lips.

I take my board up to the dry sand and put it down. Willow and Kas follow me and shyly strip off to their underwear. Kas has her arms across her chest and Willow jumps up and down to keep warm.

'We reckon the wetsuit's not fair,' Kas says. 'If we're gonna get cold, you are too.'

'All of us together,' Willow says, kicking at the sand.

So I unzip it and peel it off. I'm glad I left my jocks on underneath. Willow runs ahead but pulls up short of the waterline. Kas walks down next to me and I steal a glance at her. Her body is thin but her dark skin glows in the sun. She has a singlet on and a pair of black undies that might have been Mum's. I could be imagining it but I think she's leaning in to me as we walk. Our shoulders touch and her hair brushes against my arm. We reach Willow, who's bouncing on her toes in the shallows.

'Is it safe?' Kas asks.

The sea is second nature to me, part of who I am. I remember Dad carrying me into the water when I was really little. I could swim by the time I was five and I started going to the beach on my own when I was ten. I've never felt fear in the water, though Dad always taught me to respect it, not to take anything for granted, especially when the bigger swells are running.

'Okay,' I say, 'the waves are pretty small but there's a strong current running along the beach. You'll have to brace against it.'

I'm peering out to sea and when I look back at Kas and Willow I can tell they haven't understood a word. So I hold out my hands and they each take one.

'Come on,' I say, and we walk out until the white water pushes against our knees. The water is freezing and I can feel the goosebumps rising all over my skin. Willow grabs hold of my arm with both hands, while Kas lets go and edges back towards the beach, looking uncertain.

'Take Wils first,' she says, 'I'll wait here.'

Willow climbs onto my back and we walk out to where the waves are breaking on the bar. She seems so much bigger and heavier now than a few months ago. The current is strong but I hold my footing and before long we are pushing through chest-high waves. Willow's squealing with the excitement of it, her arms squeezed around my neck hard enough for it to hurt. Slowly, she slips off and dives under a wave.

After a few minutes she's shaking with the cold so I guide her back in to where Kas is standing in the shallows. Willow runs up the beach to dry off and Rowdy follows her.

Kas looks at me with wide eyes. I mean really looks at me,

like she hasn't since Rose died. She takes my hand and we turn to walk out into the waves. By the time we get to the bar she's bracing her body against the sweep.

When a bigger wave pushes through, she turns her back and it knocks her off her feet.

I show her how to dive under them and before long she's sliding through the water like she's been doing it all her life. When she surfaces her hair is a slick of black down her back. Her mother's ring, looped around her neck on a strip of leather, falls out of her singlet.

'Okay,' I say, 'try this now.'

I pick up a wave and body surf it a few metres towards the beach. She can't quite get the hang of it at first but eventually she throws herself down the face of a smallish wave and comes up spluttering next to me. She surprises me by standing and hugging me. Her skin is cold and I hold her, not quite sure what's going on. Her breath comes in sharp little pants and when she lifts her head I see she is crying, her body jerking with the effort. I'm so surprised, I don't know how to react. I thought we were having fun.

'I'm sorry,' she says, her voice shaking. 'I'm so sorry, Finn.'

'Sorry for what?'

'Shutting you out.'

'It's okay, Kas. She was your sister.'

'And your friend.'

Her eyes are red from the crying and the salt.

I don't see the next wave coming. It bowls us over and we roll across the bar, a tangle of arms and legs. Kas throws her hair back and grabs my hand.

Willow is huddled in the pile of clothes further up the beach. She stands and runs down to meet us. Kas nuzzles into her neck and hair, and kisses her. Willow puts her arms around Kas and the three of us stagger and fall in a heap on the dry sand. Rowdy dances around and barks excitedly.

'I'm sorry to you, too, Wils,' Kas says. She is still hanging on to me, our wet skin covered in sand. We get to our feet, link arms and walk back into the water to wash off. With Kas and Willow rolling over each other in the shallows, I would've taken a photo of this back before the virus. Moments like this are so rare now, when we forget about surviving and actually enjoy ourselves. When I think about everything we've lost— our families, our friends, our homes—it's easy to forget about what we'd be doing if the virus hadn't swept them all away. I'd be in senior school, playing football, surfing whenever I could and living with Mum and Dad. Willow would be with Harry and Stella where she belongs, and maybe even Kas would have a better life, living with Stan and Beth and Rose, riding Yogi and working on the farm.

I look at them now and try to hold onto the smiles on their faces before we go back to the business of staying alive.

We make our way up to the platform, where I stash my board and wetsuit in the bushes and throw on a warm jumper. The wind is stronger up here and it pricks at our skin. Kas leads the way and Willow and I follow. Rowdy has raced ahead. I find I'm looking at Kas. I watch the way her calf muscles flex with every step and her hair swings behind her, all wet and tangled. She turns and walks backwards for a while, a smile easing its way across her face.

She doesn't say anything, but she laughs and the sound rings around inside me.

3

Dinner tonight feels totally different. Willow and I don't have to edge our way around Kas, we don't have to coax her into talking or try to convince her to eat. Whatever decision she's come to, we're grateful for it because we've been carrying her these last few months. And there's no room for passengers. I'm hoping she will hunt with us now, that she'll help more with picking the mussels off the reef, even plant some of our stored seed in the veggie garden.

After dinner, Kas sits and reads with Willow, the two of them tucked up under blankets on the couch. Kas is more patient than I am. She doesn't race ahead or get frustrated when

Willow forgets words. Eventually Kas's voice drops away. She strokes Willow's blonde curls and glances up at me. There's a look of contentedness on her face. Willow sways off down the hall to bed. Kas sits close to the fire.

'We need to talk,' she says.

'What about?'

She gives me one of those looks that reminds me of Rose— her lips pressed together as though she knows exactly what she wants to say but is unsure of how to say it.

'We've been kept safe here by the winter. We haven't seen Wilders since we left Ray's place the day—'

'But?'

'They'll come back for us. For me. They'll find us eventually. And that means they'll find our stores, too.'

'I've been thinking about the same thing for a while now. You just weren't there.' This isn't quite true—I've pushed the idea to the back of my mind for months.

'I'm sorry,' she says. There is a hint of anger in her voice. 'But I'm back now.' She reaches over and holds me by the wrists. 'I'm back.'

'I couldn't get through to you, Kas. I tried. I really tried.'

'I felt it. But you were giving up on me, too. Both of you.'

'We had to hunt. We had to fish. We had to keep us fed.' I know I sound defensive, but I can't help it.

'You seemed to be carrying on like nothing had happened. To Rose, I mean. But all I felt was this huge emptiness. I wanted to reach out to you but you shut me down.' There are tears welling in her eyes. One escapes and she swipes it away. 'I wanted you to comfort me but it felt like you just wanted to kiss me and that's not what I needed.'

She's turning this onto me, like it's my fault. I lean back in my chair and cross my arms. I can't look at her. If it wasn't for me and Willow we would've starved by now. We'd have had no wood to burn if we hadn't collected it, no water in the header tank if I hadn't pumped it up by hand.

Kas kneels in front of me, her back to the fire. I try to look past her but she follows me with her eyes. Then, slowly, she leans forward and touches my cheek. 'Truce?' she says.

'Truce.'

She gets up and sits on the arm of the chair. She puts her lips to my ear and says, 'I missed you.'

I can feel my face go red.

While I struggle to find the words for how I feel, she slides off the chair onto the floor and sits cross-legged, her hands reaching out to the fire again.

'What do you think we should do?' I ask. 'About the spring. The summer. Staying safe.'

'We can survive in Angowrie,' she says. 'We can hunt, fish, grow veggies. Our supplies are here. But we've got to make it safe.'

The heat from the fire has made her birthmark more notice-able. It rises like a dark map on the side of her face.

'And I made a promise to Rose. To find Hope and bring her home.' She pauses and looks straight at me, defiant. 'We have to go to Longley,' she says.

I've known this was coming since that first night back from

Ray's when Kas was angry and exhausted and said she wanted to hunt Ramage down, but I've tried not to think about it. 'Travelling into Wilder country would be so dangerous. And what about Willow? We couldn't take her with us.'

'We could take her home, first. Think about it, Finn. We don't know what happened in the valley after we escaped but, either way, Harry and the farmers will be in the same position as us, living in fear of Ramage. With their help, we could maybe attack Longley.'

'Hang on! *Attack?*' I can't believe what I'm hearing. 'I thought we were going to find Hope.'

'We are, but have you forgotten what Ramage did to Rose?'

'Course I haven't. But what if Ramage controls the valley? What do we do then?'

'I don't know. But if we're smart about it we could stop the Wilders being a threat for good.' She pauses then, waiting for my response.

'It's a long shot, Kas.'

'I know. But what's the alternative? Sitting here jumping at shadows, waiting for them to come and find us. I don't want to live like that.'

All the softness has left her and in its place is the fierceness I first saw at the meeting in the valley when she attacked Tusker.

'And as for Willow,' she says. 'She deserves to be back with Harry and Stella.'

'But we escaped from the valley. They wanted to hold us prisoner. Why do you think anything would have changed?'

'That was before Ramage found them, when they thought

they were safe. They'll know they're not now, if they haven't been overrun altogether.'

What she's saying makes sense, but we're okay here at the moment. We're actually starting to enjoy ourselves a little bit. Today at the beach was really special. If we were careful, stayed low and never allowed them to see us, maybe Ramage and his men would leave us alone. But even as I build this argument in my head, I know it's not realistic. They could come and burn the town to the ground just to spite us.

She follows my eyes again, not letting me get away with avoiding a decision. 'You know doing nothing isn't an option, Finn. We have to leave Angowrie one way or another.'

She's right but I'm too tired to think.

'Let me sleep on it,' I say, getting to my feet.

'Sure,' she says, her voice lower and softer. 'But I remember something else.'

'What?'

'You promised Rose, too. I heard you.'

4

Maybe it's exhaustion from everything that happened yesterday, but I oversleep. The sun is streaming in through the curtains and I know the wind is up from the cypress rustling against the spouting outside my window. Kas is standing in the doorway, her hip pushed to one side. She's wearing an old woollen jumper of Dad's and shorts. She holds a cup of hot water to her lips and the steam curls around her face.

'How'd you sleep?' she asks.

'On and off. You?'

'Okay.'

I bunch the pillow behind me and sit up, holding my breath

to make my chest look bigger. Eventually I have to breathe out, though.

She comes and sits next to me, putting the cup on the bedside table. 'Sorry about last night,' she says. 'I didn't mean to be so pushy.'

Willow walks through the door, rubbing her eyes and yawning. 'Come here, sleepyhead,' Kas says and Willow puts her arms around her.

This is how we should be able to live, just the three of us looking out for each other. But my mind swings back to our conversation from last night, the one about leaving Angowrie. I know Kas will bring it up again.

Willow has become our egg collector. She's named all the chooks and they're so used to her, they follow her around. Yesterday she brought home another six eggs, so we cook them for breakfast. Kas looks at me across the table and smiles. Willow jigs up and down, eager to get outside. The weather is warm again today and I'm guessing she will want to go for another swim.

Kas puts her knife and fork carefully on her empty plate and says, 'So, you know what we talked about last night?' Her eyes widen and I know she wants to bring Willow into the discussion.

'Yeah,' I say.

'Have you thought about it?'

Willow pipes up. 'Thought about what?'

I nod to Kas.

'Now it's getting warmer, we reckon the Wilders'll come looking for us again. And,' Kas continues, 'we might have to leave Angowrie.' She says this slowly, looking at Willow for her reaction.

'Where would we go?' Willow asks, her face screwed up, sceptical.

Somehow it seems the decision has already been made about leaving.

I push the last of my eggs around on my plate, just long enough for her to see I know what she's doing. 'We'll go out and see Ray first. But then—' I hesitate, as though by saying it out loud it becomes final. 'Then, we'll make our way to the valley. Back to Stella and Harry.'

Willow jumps out of her seat. 'Home?' she says. 'Home? To Mum and Dad.' I can almost see her mind ticking. 'We'll have to check the traps first,' she says, working through a list in her head. 'And have another swim and get some more eggs and lock up the stores and pack some clothes and…'

Her enthusiasm is infectious. Kas and I both smile at her excitement.

Leaving is more Kas's decision than mine but I don't have a better plan. And, in the back of my mind, there's the promise we both made to Rose.

'There's something else,' Kas says after Willow has gone to start packing. 'We can't leave the house like this. If they find it, they'll know we've been living here and they'll look for the stores.'

'So, what are you saying?'

'We need to make the place look deserted, like all the others. We should take everything we need to keep and put it in with the stores. Then we'll trash the house, just enough to make it look as though it was ransacked after the virus: cupboards open, stuff spilled on the floor, chairs thrown around, beds turned over, doors open.'

I know she's right but this is our home, or the closest thing to it I've had in three winters.

'Don't worry,' she says, 'We'll clean it up when we get back.'

It takes us two days to get organised. I know I'm stalling, but I convince Kas we have to plan carefully. We're going to miss having Yogi. He made carrying food and gear so much easier. Kas is looking forward to seeing him again out at Ray's place. In the meantime, though, we bring supplies in from the garage and spread them on the floor. Along with the food—cans of beans and sardines—we've got to carry sleeping bags, the bow and arrows, a couple of knives, the can opener, extra clothes, the torch, batteries and matches. We bundle everything into food bags and thread pieces of rope through loops at the top so we can sling them over our shoulders. They'll be uncomfortable but we don't have a choice.

The next day we strip out the house. Everything that's valuable—the bedding and mattresses, the kitchen stuff, the three best chairs, the cushions off the couch—it all goes into the garage with the food stores. Then we arrange everything else to look like the house has been trashed, the kitchen table turned over, drawers pulled out, cupboards opened, the couch lying on its back. Kas even brings in shovel-loads of dirt and leaves from the garden and spreads them around the floor. By the time we're finished it looks nothing like our home, which is exactly the effect we were aiming for. Finally, we stand out in the yard and look at our handiwork. Rowdy is confused. He doesn't understand why we upset his bed in the corner and threw his smelly old blanket over the upturned table.

'There's something wrong,' Kas says.

'What?'

'Sorry, Finn, but we're going to have to smash some windows. It's too'—she searches for the word—'intact.'

So we choose a window each and gather up rocks to throw. Willow is excited. She's never done anything like this before.

'Let's think about which ones to break,' I say. 'We're not going to be able to replace them when we get back.'

I choose a window out the front, Kas takes one on the side and Willow picks a lower one in the lounge room. We throw our rocks and the sound of smashing glass fills the air. Rowdy barks, more confused than ever.

When we finish we reward ourselves with a swim, heading to the beach about an hour before sunset, while there's still some warmth in the air. The swell has dropped back and it's easy for me to stroke out beyond the bar. Kas and Willow stay in waist-deep water, diving under the small waves and popping up to look out towards me. Eventually I catch a wave back to them, grabbing Kas's leg under the water. When I surface she slaps my hand away but when I turn my back she jumps on me and pulls me under. I can't remember ever feeling like this before, this thrill of being close to someone.

It's almost dark by the time we trudge back up the dunes. At the top, we look back at the river mouth one last time. What we see when we turn towards home takes our breath away. The sky above the ridge that rims the town is lit by four fires, maybe a half a kilometre apart. Four beacons. Four warnings.

We're no longer alone.

We drop to the ground, unsure of whether we've been seen. Kas sticks her head above the tussock grass and looks again.

'*Shit!*' she says.

Keeping low, we make our way down the track towards the beach road, cross it quickly and reach the trail through to Parker Street. There's something uncomfortably familiar about the feeling of adrenaline pumping through my body. It's not something I've missed these past few months.

We take cover behind the shed. I hold Rowdy by the collar and check that everything's okay before running across the yard to the safety of the house. We lock ourselves in and close every curtain. It's dark inside but our eyes slowly adjust until we can make each other out.

'Well, that changes things,' Kas says, one hand raking through her hair.

Something doesn't make sense to me. 'It's weird,' I say. 'If it's Wilders, why wouldn't they come quietly and catch us off guard?'

'Maybe they're trying to flush us out,' Kas says.

'Are we still going to the valley?' Willow asks. Kas and I exchange glances. I'm pretty sure we're both thinking the same thing—we have to leave. And soon.

'We're packed already. We could go tonight,' Kas says.

But she hasn't been out in the bush like Willow and I have—she hasn't seen the storm damage. It'd be impossible to find our way in the dark.

'Too hard,' I say. 'I reckon we hold off till first light.'

'They could be waiting for us up there. Any number of them,' Kas says. 'I knew we should have left earlier. You stalled us too long. Now look what's happened.'

There's a tense silence. Maybe she's right. Maybe this is my fault.

Willow is looking from one of us to the other. 'No use arguing about it,' she says, sounding just like Stella. 'How do we get out of here without being caught?'

'I know the tracks better than anybody,' I say, happy to move on from laying blame.

Kas seems to have moved on too. 'Where do you reckon the fires were exactly?' she asks.

'I'm not sure but we've got traps set up on the fence and we need some meat for the journey. We'll go there first.'

Kas is shaking her head. 'You're kidding?' she says. 'We might as well give ourselves up.'

'Come on, Kas. They're trying to spook us into running, showing ourselves. We could circle further west before we climb up to the ridge, get around behind them.'

She thinks for a while. 'It's a risk we don't have to take.'

'It's not only the rabbits. We need the traps. We can't afford to lose them.'

I get the feeling she can see I'm right. Besides, I'm the only one who can navigate; Willow's never been the way we'll have to travel now.

'First light, then,' Kas says. 'Now, we need to sleep.'

'We should have someone keeping watch, I say. 'I'll go first.' I don't tell them I'm so wired I couldn't sleep anyway.

We open some beans and eat enough to keep the hunger pangs at bay through the night.

After Willow and Kas have bedded down on the floor, I slip out the back with Rowdy and retrace our steps to the platform. The fires are still burning. They look bigger and brighter, but I figure that's because it's darker now. I stand up on the railing to get a better view and, taking my bearings from the river, note each one's location. And something strikes me as strange—they're different sizes. The further west, the smaller the fire. I think I know why.

There is one problem, though—I'm pretty sure one of them is close to the hayshed.

It's barely light when we walk out past the grove of sheoaks to Parker Street. We need to head around the western edge of the golf course, swinging as wide as we can through the scrub before we climb towards the ridge. The tracks out here are more like riverbeds—we have to pick our way along them. Kas and I walk all the more carefully with the bags. Willow has the bow over her shoulder and the arrows in a stopped piece of plastic pipe looped through her belt. Every ten metres or so there is debris blocking our way. The bush is eerily quiet—the wind hardly stirs the leaves, as though everything is finding its breath again after the storms. It takes us a couple of hours to get up to the ridge, and another hour to make our way in a wide arc to the hayshed. By the time we reach the paddocks the sun is fully up.

I was right—over in the furthest corner of the paddock, not far from the gate where I knocked Ramage off his bike, smoke rises from the remains of a fire.

'I don't like it,' Kas says. 'We should go straight to Ray's.'

But I'm not giving up my traps that easily. 'Unless we want to run across the open paddock, we've gotta stick close to the fence anyway. We can pick up the traps as we go.'

'Shit, you're stubborn!' she says.

'I wouldn't be alive if I wasn't.'

We move back into the bush and, staying low, head south towards the fence. The first trap is empty but it hasn't been sprung. While Kas keeps guard and Willow holds an arrow tight in her bow, I crawl out of the bush, spring the trap with a stick and pull it out of the ground. It all happens in a matter of seconds and I'm back in the cover of the trees. The next two traps are also empty, but in the last one, closest to the gate— and the smouldering fire—is a rabbit, its back leg caught in the metal jaws, its eyes blinking.

Willow signals to me to take the bow. Kas shakes her head, but I know Willow can do this. She darts out, frees the rabbit and quickly stretches its neck, before pulling up the trap and scuttling back to Kas and me.

She pulls a piece of twine from her pocket and binds its feet.

'You two have got the bags,' she says. 'I'll carry this.'

'Where did you learn that?' Kas asks, shaking her head.

'Finn,' Willow says.

I hide the traps in the hollow log I've used before. Then we stop and take stock.

'There's no one here,' Kas says. 'That fire hasn't been tended for hours.'

'That makes sense,' I say. I tell them about my walk up to the platform last night. 'One thing got me thinking—why four fires? Why not just one?'

'And?'

'If it's Wilders, they want us to think there are more of them than there really are. The fires were all different sizes.'

'So?'

'They were all lit by the same person and it took them a while to move from one spot to the next.'

Willow's onto it, now. 'So by the time they got to the last one, the first one was burning down.'

'Okay, but there must still be someone up here, somewhere,' Kas says. 'We need to get out to Ray's as quick as we can.'

We pick our way back down the ridge to the road that heads east towards Ray's, feeling the weight of our loads, but saying nothing.

We stop to rest once we get to the road junction leading up to Pinchgut. We have to be super careful down here. It's tough going though. When we swing east along the coast road we see the roof of a shed that's been ripped off and blown halfway across a paddock.

But there are signs of new life, too. The bush is alive with wildflowers, pinks and purples and bright yellows and the last of the wattle blossoms.

I notice Kas is dropping back, choosing to walk on her own while Willow and I keep up a steady pace, Rowdy at our heels. Her head is down and there's no purpose in her step. I touch Willow on the shoulder and we stop to wait for Kas.

'What's up?' I ask.

She turns away. 'Rose,' she says quietly.

Shit, of course. I've been so caught up in getting ready to leave, planning the trip and making sure everything is locked up and safe, I've forgotten we haven't been out to Ray's since Rose died. I take Kas's hand and gently pull her forward.

'It's hard,' I say, 'but we've gotta do it sometime. It might as well be now.'

The sun drops early, with spring not quite holding its own yet. It's taken most of the day to get to the top of Ray's valley. We've walked through the bush parallel to the road, climbing over and through debris. It's exhausting. The light is falling away as we finally wind down the rough track to Ray's top paddock. There's not much wind but I pick up a faint smell of smoke. As we get closer, I realise the smell is much stronger than a fire burning in a stove.

We stumble out of the bush and stop.

Across the paddock is the glow of a large fire that looks like it's been burning for a while. My heart stops. The slope of the land means we can't quite see where it's coming from, but I know its Ray's house. I move to jump the fence. Kas grabs me by the arm.

'Wait,' she says, panic in her voice.

She pulls us into the bush and we use the trees as cover, making our way to the corner of the paddock. Here we drop down with the lie of the land until we're level with the house. Or where the house used to be. There's nothing left but a crumple of roofing iron and charred timbers. In the middle, the coals glow orange.

There's no sign of Ray. Kas has her hands to her mouth and Willow stands beside her, staring through the wire.

As the sun drops behind the trees, the coals glow brighter.

The shed in the home paddock is close enough to the tree line to get to without being spotted. We follow the fence downhill until we are about twenty metres from the shed.

'I'll go first and give you a signal if it's all clear,' I say. Kas and Willow nod, their eyes fixed on the remains of the house.

Leaving my sack with them, I slide through the fence wires and run as quickly as I can to the side of the shed. There is another smell here, something different from the smell of the fire, but I can't quite figure it out. I should have brought the torch with me so I could check inside the shed, but it's quiet so I whistle to Kas and Willow. Kas comes first, holding Rowdy by the collar to stop him bolting. Willow is behind them.

Just as they get to me a deep voice makes me jump.

'Well, well,' the voice says. 'What've we got here?'

Two dark shapes appear out of the shed.

Wilders.

5

The man on my right strikes a match and lights a kero lamp. He lifts it above his head and pushes it towards us.

'Well, I'll be fucked,' the other one says. 'If it isn't the ugly sister. I remember you.'

He sticks out his big paw and grabs Kas, pulling her towards him. She tries to shake him off, but he's twice her size.

He holds her at arm's length and says, 'Feisty like your sister, too.'

The one holding the lantern brings it to my face, close enough I can feel its heat. His hair is long and straggly and it's hard to tell where the hair ends and his beard starts. He smells like shit.

'And this is the little prick we been chasin' since last summer, isn't it, Gauge?'

He leans in even closer, smiles and says, 'You're well and truly stuffed, boy. You nearly killed Ramage with that wire across the gate. You got a price on your head and me and Gauge, we're gonna collect.'

Willow has been hiding behind Kas but the one with the lantern has spotted her. 'And another girlie here, too,' he says laughing. 'Well, haven't we hit the jackpot. We're gonna be rich, Gauge.'

'I knew it, Birch. I knew the fires would spook 'em. Couldn't help 'emselves, I reckon, worryin' about the old man, thinkin' about the dead girl,' Gauge says.

He's holding Kas by the hair now, with his other arm around her neck. She's trying to brace herself to push away from him but it's having no affect.

'Where's Ray?' It hardly sounds like me talking, my voice shakes so much.

Birch barks like a dog, then starts to laugh, pointing at the remains of the house. 'A bit slow, the old fella. Then again, when you're tied to a chair it's hard to move real quick.'

I swing a punch with everything I've got and connect below his ribs but it bounces off him. In an instant he lifts me by my jumper and pushes me against the wall of the shed.

'You'll have to hit harder than that, son,' he says. He slams a fist into my stomach and knocks the wind out of me. I crumple to the ground gasping for breath. Willow throws herself on top of me.

Birch reaches down and hauls her up by the arm.

'You'll bring a good price back in Longley too, girlie.'

Birch picks me up and pushes Willow and me into Kas. I feel rope being tied around my wrists behind my back. Birch starts to tie Kas, but Gauge stops him.

'Not yet, Birchy.' He licks his lips and smiles through rotted teeth. 'Haven't seen a girl in months,' he says.

Birch laughs.

'You look after these two,' Gauge says, dragging Kas into the shed by her hair.

'Wanna bag ta put over her head?' Birch shouts after him.

Willow is cowering against me, pushing her head into my chest. We've been shoved onto the ground. Birch has seen Rowdy and he starts making clicking noises with his tongue, trying to win him over. Rowdy growls and backs away.

Everything is quiet. The lamp casts a huge shadow of Birch against the shed wall. I can't hear Kas at all—no screams, no noise of a struggle—and the silence makes me sick.

Frantic now, I work at the rope around my wrists, twisting and pulling. I can feel blood trickling into my hands. Finally, I slip free. I'm watching Birch kneeling on the ground, all his attention focused on Rowdy, when a figure rises behind him. It's Kas. She lifts a piece of wood the size of a baseball bat and brings it crashing down on Birch's head. There's the sound of bone cracking and the kero lamp hissing where it falls into the damp grass. Birch is thrown forward by the blow, his neck snapping back as he hits the ground. Kas lifts the wood again and brings it down on the back of his head. Then again and again. I cover Willow's face, but she knows what's happening.

Kas is yelling with every blow, a wild howl, filled with tears and hate.

'Ugly bitch. Ugly bitch,' she says over and over.

I get to my feet. 'Kas', I say. 'Enough. It's enough, now.'

When I grab her arm and take the piece of wood, she slumps to her knees and pounds the dirt with her fist. Her body heaves and shakes. When I reach out and touch her shoulder she brings her hand up to hold mine. It's sticky with blood.

'What happened?' I whisper, trying to see back into the shed.

She shakes her head and looks away. The moonlight reflects off the blade of a knife on the ground. It's one of the kitchen knives I packed before we left and it's covered in blood right up to the handle. I squat down and put my arms around her, holding her until her body is still.

After a minute or so, she shrugs me off and stands up. She takes a deep breath and looks at us. Her chin is up and I hardly recognise her voice.

'No one hurts me,' she says. 'No one.'

She wipes her hands on the grass before picking up the knife, cleaning it in the same way and sliding it into her belt.

I lift the lantern that Birch has dropped. His body is a formless lump in the dark. There's blood on the handle of the lantern but the wick has somehow stayed alight. Holding it up I see Willow cowering against the wall of the shed. Kas has walked off a few metres and is bent over, vomiting.

I go to Willow. 'Wils, it's over now. It's all over,' I say.

'Is Kas all right?' Her voice quivers.

'She'll be okay,' I say, hoping I'm right.

'Did he hurt her?'

'I don't know. But he can't hurt us anymore.'

I put the lamp on the ground and crouch in front of her.

'I was scared, Finn,' she says.

'Yeah, me too.' I try to hold my voice steady but I'm shaking all over.

Kas walks over to us, wiping her mouth.

I look at her closely, trying to see if she's hurt, but her eyes are glazed over. It'll be a while before she talks about what happened in the shed.

I try not to think about Ray, but I can't stop myself—his funny bow-legged walk, his way of making me feel at home. I can't believe he's gone. Not like that. Not in his own home. Kas sits and the three of us hold each other tight.

We take the lantern and walk across the home paddock to what's left of the house. It's still giving off heat even though it looks like it's been burning for days. I can't bear to think of Ray in there somewhere, the remains of him. We move around the outside of the fire, looking for anything recognisable, but everything is buried under the hot sheets of corrugated iron that used to be the roof. I think of the time I spent out here with Ray the winter after Mum died. He took me in, saved me, really, just in the way he went about things, slow and deliberate. He never lectured me, never told me what to do.

Kas is behind me. She loops her arms around my waist, the point of her chin touching my back. Every now and again a spasm rocks her body.

'Why does everyone I'm close to have to die?' she says.

I don't have an answer for her. Willow presses against my side and the three us stand there, hardly wanting to acknowledge the way the heat of the fire warms our bodies.

'What now?' Kas asks.

'We have to find somewhere to sleep. The shed's the only protection we'll get from the cold. You wait here with Wils and I'll go and clean it up a bit.'

Kas doesn't answer, but she takes Willow by the hand and leads her to the other side of the fire. It's eerily quiet when I get back to the shed. I start with Birch, the one outside. I don't want to see his face so I hook the lantern on a nail and grab him by the legs. He's heavier than I expected. His boots come loose in my hands so I pull them off and try to hold him around the ankles. Gradually I inch him around the back where the grass is longer. With one last heave I manage to roll him a little way down the hill and he comes to rest against a clump of weeds.

Inside, I find Gauge lying awkwardly against a workbench. It looks as though he's tried to prop himself up but his head hangs to the side and the whole front of his body, his shirt and his pants, is covered in blood. I can't see the wound and I don't want to. I have to drag him by the feet too, his head bumping along on the uneven floor. He's not as heavy as Birch, and pretty soon they are both lying in the grass at the back of the shed. I think about checking their pulses but I don't really care if they breathe their last breaths out here in the cold in the middle of the night.

I whistle to Kas and Willow. They've made their way to the fence to pick up the sacks and they appear out of the dark. There's a small hayloft in the shed that has some dry bales in it, so I break them open to make a bed. In all the adrenaline rush I've almost forgotten how hungry I am. Willow and I gut and skin the rabbit while Kas takes a shovel to get some hot coals from the fire. Before long, we've got our own fire going just inside the door of the shed and I've rigged a spit to cook the rabbit. No one says anything, but Kas looks back into the dark where Gauge was. I can't read her expression in the flickering light of the fire. Fat drops into the flames and it spits and crackles.

Kas finally speaks, her voice low and lonely. 'Maybe this is what the world is now.' She pokes at the fire with a stick. 'Ramage, people like him, they know there're no rules anymore, no one to stop them doing whatever they want.' She breathes in deep, lifts her head and adds, 'We have to be as cruel as them.'

'Not everyone's like the Wilders,' I say. 'What about Harry and Stella and the others in the valley? They're like us.'

'Some were. Not all of them.'

I'd forgotten about Tusker.

'Mum and Dad,' Willow says, 'I miss them so much.'

Kas puts an arm around her shoulders. 'I know, Wils. You're lucky to have them.' She stops there but I can see she wants to say more. Her eyes pierce the dark and shoot straight through me.

'Anyway,' I say, 'we don't know if Ray was in the house. We've only got the Wilders' word for it and I wouldn't trust anything they say. He might've escaped.'

Kas says nothing.

'We'll have a good look around in the morning. He could've taken off into the bush and waited for them to leave,' I say.

'First thing we have to do in the morning,' Kas says, 'is find Rose's grave.'

'And Yogi,' Willow says. 'Don't forget about Yogi.'

This brings a smile to Kas's face and she looks out into the dark as if she might see him there.

The rabbit is charred now so I pull it off the spit and cut it into pieces. It's pretty raw on the inside but we are so hungry we hardly notice. All three of us lean into the fire, tearing the meat from the bone and chewing loudly. I give a piece to Rowdy. Kas breaks the bones open and sucks the marrow out, just like I remember Rose doing on the first night she arrived in Angowrie. That feels like a lifetime ago.

Willow is the first to climb up into the hayloft. We've laid out the sleeping bags on the loose hay. Kas and I stay by the fire. She shifts around until she's sitting next to me and after a while she lies down and rests her head in my lap. I touch her cheek and brush the hair away from her face.

'You okay?' I ask. Her body stiffens a little and her head rises slightly out of my lap.

'Kinda,' she says.

'What happened in the shed?'

She shakes her head and I see her lip quiver.

'Sorry,' I say.

'It's okay. He didn't get near me. He didn't even see the knife.

It was all so quick.' She lifts her hand and strokes my arm. 'I should feel something. But I don't. I don't feel anything.'

'You're in shock.'

'No, I mean I don't feel bad about it. They were going to harm us. And they've already killed Ray, and one way or another Rose, too. They deserved it.'

I look closely at her face. Her eyes burn.

'I feel like I've been angry my whole life,' she says. 'Treated like shit for as long as I can remember. It's turned me into someone I never thought I'd be.'

'None of that's your fault, Kas. It's all stuff you had no control over.'

She hesitates and shifts her position a little. 'You know you're the best thing that's ever happened to me.'

'What about Stan and Beth?'

'They were okay, especially Stan. But when it came down to it, we were still their property.'

'Rose didn't say much about them but I got the idea she liked them.'

'She and Beth were close. I did more work in the paddocks with Stan, riding the horses.'

She's rested her head back down into my lap. I'm so tired I can hardly move.

'We need to sleep,' I say.

'I meant what I said. You're the best thing that's happened to me. When I'm with you I'm not just'—she hesitates a moment—'not just a Siley.'

I know what she's saying but I was hoping she meant

something more than that.

We climb the ladder to the loft. Willow has spread herself across the middle of the straw so I lift her to one side and make room. Kas snuggles up against me and I listen to her steady breath. I lie awake thinking of what I will do if the time comes for me to protect the people I love. Will I be as fierce and brave as Kas or will it be like the time I had the chance to kill Ramage? Will I back away and leave the dirty work to someone else?

The morning cold creeps into the shed. Outside, mist hovers just above the ground. Willow has rolled over during the night and she's warm against my side. I feel for Kas but her sleeping bag is empty. I need to piss so I slip out, pull my boots on without bothering with the laces and climb down the ladder. I walk around the side of the shed and piss against the corrugated iron wall. Looking up towards the remains of the house I spy Kas standing under a tree in the corner of the home paddock. Her back is turned and she's looking down. I know what she's found.

I tie my laces, pull on a jumper and walk up the hill towards Kas. The wreck of the house still smoulders but it's giving off less heat than it was last night. Kas is crouching down, with her hands resting on the mound in front of her. I stop a few paces behind her.

'Rose?'

She nods her head slowly.

There's no marking on the grave and the spring grass has

crept up onto the raised bed.

'I looked all around,' she says. 'There's nothing else. This must be her.'

I take a few steps forward and squat beside her.

'I don't think I've got any tears left,' she says.

The morning sun breaks through the trees and steam rises off the paddock.

'She was more than my sister. She was my whole family, all of it. Since we left Pakistan there's only ever been the two of us and we had to be everybody to each other.'

'When Rose came to Angowrie all she could talk about was you being out there on your own, how she needed to look after you,' I say.

'I have this memory, Finn, the earliest thing I can remember. I don't know where it was but we were in a crowd, people pushing and shoving, trying to get through a gate with high fences either side of it. Everyone was bigger than us and all I could see were legs and boots and bags. Rose was holding my hand, pulling me through little gaps she made in the crowd. But someone stood on my foot and my hand slipped out of hers. She had these green plastic boots on and I could see her getting swept away from me. I kept moving but I was pressed harder and harder from every side. I couldn't breathe. When I'd just got through the gate I felt a hand grab my arm and pull me to the side. It was Rose and she was angry. She slapped me across the face and told me never to do anything like that again, like it was my fault. But then she hugged me and when I looked at her she was crying. "I thought I'd lost you," she said. Then there was gunfire and gas that made our eyes sting. That's all I remember.'

Kas wraps her arms around her knees and rocks back and forth. 'She deserved so much more than this. Why couldn't she find just a little bit of happiness?'

'I saw her smile. She even cracked jokes and told me I was too skinny. Called me dog boy. I think she knew what happiness was.'

Kas looks at me with sadness in her eyes.

'And it doesn't mean you can't he happy,' I say.

She doesn't answer but she stands up and hugs me.

We turn then and walk back down the paddock. Willow is standing in the shed door, shading her eyes with one arm and waving with the other. Rowdy is beside her. Kas looks back up towards the grave. 'We need to make something to put on it,' she says. 'To show where she is.'

Breakfast is beans heated on the fire and some eggs. I'd forgotten about Ray's chooks but Willow found two of them sitting on a nest in the hay. Rowdy lies in the sunshine crunching on the rabbit bones from last night.

There was a billycan in the shed that must have belonged to the Wilders.

'They hadn't been here long, those two,' Kas says. 'There's no bedding, no food, unless they lost it in the fire or stashed it somewhere else. We should have a look around.'

'Did you find Yogi, Kas?' Willow says.

'No, I looked everywhere. I think he's gone.'

'But he's alive?'

48

'Maybe. He's tough. We'll probably find him out in the bush somewhere.'

We pack up our belongings and take the Wilders' billycan too. I can't help looking behind the shed. Gauge and Birch are both exactly where I left them last night. We don't have time to bury them, anyway.

Kas leads us back up the paddock to the grave.

'Wils, let's collect some flowers,' she says.

'Do you want me to rig up something to mark the grave?' I ask.

She thinks about this for a few seconds then says, 'I s'pose so. Maybe a pile of rocks?'

Kas and Willow slip through the fence and start to pick the wildflowers growing along the edge of the bush while I look for some rocks. By the time I've collected enough for a small cairn, Kas and Willow have woven their flowers into a wreath. The rocks look pretty rough but I figure Rose wouldn't mind. Willow rests the wreath against them.

'Should we say some sort of prayer?' I say.

'Who to?' Kas says. There's anger in her voice. 'How could any god allow this to happen?'

She kneels down and presses her cheek flat on the grave and whispers something too low to hear. Her mother's ring falls out of her shirt. She kisses it, then takes the loop of leather from around her neck and pushes the ring between the rocks, into the soft dirt. Then, she picks up her sack and starts to walk back towards the other corner of the paddock.

It doesn't feel right not to say something.

'Rest in peace, Rose,' is all I can think of. When I turn to Willow she's got her palms clasped in front of her chest and her eyes closed.

'Amen,' she says.

'Amen,' I say.

6

Once we're back in the trees we follow the track up towards the main road, Kas walking ahead of Willow and me, with Rowdy behind, sniffing the ground as he goes. When we reach the road, Kas stops and waits for us to catch up.

'What's the plan?' she asks, sitting on the trunk of an uprooted wattle.

'Nothing's changed as far as I can see,' I say. 'We head towards Pinchgut and take the track to the logging coup at the top of the ridge.'

'I'm worried there might be more Wilders,' Kas says, looking along the road. 'It doesn't make sense, them not having any supplies with them, the house still burning. It's all too recent.'

'They might have been loners,' I say, 'or maybe a scouting party for Ramage.'

'They'd never have got through the storms. More likely they've been down here the whole winter.'

'So, you reckon they'd been living in Ray's house?' I don't want to think about what Ray might have been through.

'Maybe.'

'The fire could have been an accident then—all their supplies could have been inside the house when it burned.'

'I dunno, Finn, I'm guessing. But the other thing that doesn't make sense is Yogi. I know horses—they stay where there's feed, and there was plenty in Ray's paddocks. I think he was led away.'

Willow has been sitting quietly and listening. 'What about Ray?' she says.

I see where she's going. 'If it was an accident, if it happened so fast they didn't have time to get their gear out, it's pretty unlikely they'd have tied Ray up.'

'I was thinking the same thing,' Kas says.

We don't want to think about Ray being trapped in the fire. If he wasn't there when the house burned, he could be alive.

'I reckon we should chance using the road,' Kas says. 'If we get a move on, we can make it to Pinchgut tonight. We'll have a better idea of what's going on once we see whether the junction's guarded or not.'

Without another word, we pick up our sacks and start to walk. Rowdy races ahead, darting into the bush when he picks up the scent of an animal he might chase, then bouncing back out to check on us.

We walk out in the open, weaving our way through the debris on the road, alert to any sound. When we reach the intersection where we have to head north, it's tempting to turn back for Angowrie, to the comfort of home. But the ambush at Ray's has shown us how vulnerable we are. Ramage wouldn't think twice about killing me and taking Kas. We have to take the initiative. If nothing else, he won't be expecting us to be coming north towards him. Maybe, just maybe, we can catch him off guard and that might give us the chance to find Hope.

The day passes slowly. The road north is worse than the coast road. Every turn reveals another tree blocking our way, another stretch of asphalt lifted and moved by rain and, in one section, a length of fence ripped out of the ground, gate and all, and strung across the road. It's a continuous obstacle course and it wears us down. It's late afternoon by the time we start to rise into the foothills leading to Pinchgut. We're exhausted but we want to get as far as we can before nightfall. The trees on the side of the road are taller now, meaning we're moving into the denser forest, and the air is cooler. All conversation has dropped away. Willow has fallen behind Kas and me and even Rowdy has lost interest in what the bush might be hiding.

I'm so tired, I think at first I might be imagining it, but I'm sure I can smell smoke. We're too far from the fires the Wilders lit on the ridge. Kas has noticed it too. We stop and wait for Willow to catch up and then we drop back into the cover of the bush. The wind is from the north so the fire must be ahead of us.

'I'll check it out,' I say. 'Wait here.'

Willow eases herself down into the thick grass and Kas holds Rowdy by the collar so he doesn't follow me.

There's a curve in the road about fifty metres ahead and I'm pretty sure the smoke is coming from beyond it. The road rises just before the bend and then drops between two small embankments. I climb up on the left side and make my way through the bush until I'm past the bend. There are still patches of snow on the ground. I crawl to the edge of the embankment and look over. To the side of the road is a small campfire. Two tall, thin figures stand in front of it with their hands reaching out to the flames. There is something odd about them, not their size, but the way they stand. I can't figure it out. They could be Wilders but they're not like any I've seen before. The smell of cooking meat reaches me now and I make out the carcass of a kangaroo or wallaby, hanging from a tree. I watch for a few more minutes then retreat to Kas and Willow.

Kas springs to her feet. 'What is it?' she says.

'Two men and a campfire,' I say.

'Wilders?'

'I don't think so.'

'Let me look,' she says, and she sets off through the trees on the side of the road.

Kas is gone a long while and Willow and I are starting to worry, when she appears out of the gathering darkness.

'I don't think they're Wilders,' she says.

'Why not?'

'They're black. I got close enough to see.'

'Aboriginal?'

'No. African.'

'So?'

'They could be Sileys. There were Sudanese and Somalis in the processing centres.'

'What should we do?' I ask.

'If they've come from Longley they might have information we can use.'

We look at each other and I'm aware of the way we make decisions together now.

'It'll be safer for me to approach them,' I say. 'You get in position on the embankment with Willow and cover me with the bow and arrows. If I have to run, don't try to follow. As far as they'll know, I'm on my own.'

We stash the sacks in the bush and I wait for Kas and Willow to get into position. I keep Rowdy with me. He's not much protection, but they won't know that. Then, slowly, I walk up the road and round the bend. The men are still standing at the fire, both facing me, which means Kas has their backs.

They hear Rowdy's growl first. Then they focus on me. I have one hand up in a gesture of friendship but they back away from the fire and reach for something on the ground.

'I wouldn't do that if I was you.'

It's Kas, standing about ten metres behind them, the bow drawn back and an arrow aimed at the nearest one.

Things have escalated pretty quickly.

'Woah,' one of them says. 'Woah. We're not armed.' He puts his hands up and the other one does the same.

'Sit down and keep you hands on your heads,' Kas says. She sounds menacing. 'Who are you?'

'I am Gabriel and this is Tahir.'

Tahir looks angry.

'Where are you from?' I ask, checking the ground for weapons.

They both look at me strangely, trying to figure out what I'm saying.

'He asked where you're from,' Kas says.

Their attention is drawn back to her. 'Nowhere,' Tahir replies.

'What does that mean?'

'We're No-landers.'

'What's a No-lander?' I ask. They are very dark skinned and tall, at least a couple of years older than us.

'Please,' Gabriel says. 'Don't shoot.'

Kas steps towards them, keeping the arrow tight in the bow. Willow has followed her down off the bank.

'Please,' Gabriel says again. 'Have some food.' He slowly drops his hands from his head and pulls the leg of kangaroo out of the fire. He tears a strip of meat off it and offers it me. 'We have plenty,' he says, venturing a smile.

Kas isn't convinced. She stays just out of their reach, edges around next to me and says, 'You didn't answer the question. What's a No-lander?'

The glow of the fire lights Gabriel's face. His skin shines, drawn tight across high cheekbones.

'We are Sileys,' Gabriel says. 'Like you.'

'How do you know I'm a Siley?'

'Your tracking device,' he says, pointing to the back of his own hand. 'We've been looking for you—the girl with the mark on her face.'

'What?' Kas says, lowering the bow a little. 'You've been looking for me?'

'All the No-landers are looking for you.'

'How come I've never heard of you?' Kas says.

'We're not from here. When the virus came, we travelled west from the city, looking for somewhere safe. No one tracked us; they were too worried about getting sick. But no one helped us either. Every town we came to, they drove us out.'

'Us? How many of you are there?' Kas is trying to piece together their story. Me too. Willow has accepted a piece of meat from Gabriel and she stands back from the fire eating it. Gabriel winks at her and she smiles back.

'We were five, but more joined us along the way. There are fifteen of us now,' Tahir says. 'All No-landers. All Sileys.'

'Where are the rest?' I ask, looking around at the bush.

'We have a place. A deserted farm.'

'Where?' Kas is curious.

'West,' Tahir says waving his arm vaguely in the air.

'Near Longley?'

'No, we stay clear of Longley.'

'Please,' Gabriel says again. 'Sit down. It's cold. Share our fire. Eat.' There is something in the way he speaks, the way his white teeth flash in an uncertain smile, that makes me want to trust him. I look at Kas and she nods. They make room on the ground by the fire and we huddle in. Even Rowdy has relaxed. Tahir tempts him with a small piece of meat and pats him when he moves closer.

'His name's Rowdy,' I say.

'I don't know this word,' Tahir says.

'It means noisy, I guess. But it's a joke, he's a softy, really.'

Tahir looks confused.

I almost jump away from the fire when Gabriel pulls a knife from inside his boot, but he sees my panic and places it on the ground.

'To cut the meat,' he says.

I can see the wariness in Kas's eyes. She's on edge, ready to spring if she has to.

I pick up Gabriel's knife and start hacking at the meat but he places his hand over mine and says, 'Let me.'

He seems to know exactly where to cut and the meat falls away from the bone in neat lengths. I haven't eaten kangaroo in at least three years. It tastes gamier than rabbit, but it's well cooked and not too tough.

Kas eats a small piece, chewing slowly. 'What do you mean,' she asks, 'you're looking for me?'

Gabriel and Tahir exchange glances.

'We No-landers are from everywhere and nowhere,' Gabriel says. 'Some of us are from Africa, some from Asia, some have had their land swallowed by the sea, the Pacific Islanders.

All of us have come on boats.'

'I get it,' Kas says. 'You're Sileys.'

'That's not a word we use,' Gabriel says. 'It makes us slaves.'

'I was a slave,' Kas says, leaning towards the fire. 'In Longley.'

'We know,' Gabriel replies.

'For fuck's sake!' Kas has run out of patience. 'What's with all this talk about knowing me, looking for me?'

'There is a girl,' Tahir says, 'she was held prisoner in Longley. At the feedstore. She escaped, not long after you and your sister. We found her just before the winter. She was nearly dead, starving. We took her to the farm and over the winter she gradually got better. She talked about you.'

'What's her name?' Kas interrupts.

'Vashti.'

'Describe her.'

'Indian, maybe Sri Lankan, green eyes, short.'

Kas looks at me, then back at the fire. 'Okay, I know her. She knows me. So what?'

'She says if we find you, we find your sister. She says Warda is a fighter, that she will lead us.'

'But—' Willow says before Kas cuts her off.

'Wils, I'll do the talking,' she snaps.

I pull Willow in towards me.

'I don't know why Vashti would say that. Why would Warda be interested in leading your group of'—she hesitates—'No-landers?'

'Now the winter is almost passed,' Gabriel says, 'it will become dangerous for us again. We have a home on the farm and we have to protect ourselves. We have some weapons for hunting.'

He gets to his feet slowly and walks a few paces to the tree where the kangaroo is hanging. He reaches behind it and takes out a rifle, holding it by the barrel so as not to alarm us. 'We have more of these,' he says, 'and a small amount of ammunition.'

Kas is alert again, her hand reaching for the bow. I'm ready to grab Willow and run. But Gabriel walks back to the fire and hands the rifle to Kas. I'm surprised at how easily she handles it, checking to see if it's loaded, then resting it across her lap. I'm sure I remember Rose saying Stan was the only one who used the rifles on the farm.

'You and your sister,' Tahir says, 'you know the country here. You know the dangers. And you,' he says pointing at me.

'Finn.'

'Finn. You are not a Siley, are you?'

I shake my head.

'But you must know how to hunt if you have survived this long.'

'Yeah. A bit.' I say.

Willow pipes up then. 'He's the best hunter.'

I'm trying to figure out whether this is a good turn of events or not. Gabriel and Tahir seem okay but we've lied to them about Rose and we need to find Hope before the Wilders discover we're not in Angowrie anymore.

Gabriel breaks the silence. 'Where is your sister? Where is Warda?'

Kas is ready for this question. She shoots the answer back at him. 'She's down on the coast, guarding our place.'

'Will you take us to her?' Tahir asks.

'We have something we have to do first,' she says.

'And what is that?'

'We need to travel north, to find Willow's parents.'

Tahir is curious. 'And where are they?'

'North,' Kas says again, more firmly this time, challenging him not to question any further.

But Tahir persists. 'Then you can give us directions to Warda. We can travel to her on our own.'

I've had enough of this. 'I don't think so. Like you say, the world's a dangerous place these days. We all need to be careful. We're no different from you.'

This is a stalemate built on lies, ours and theirs. If the conversation keeps going, cracks will appear.

I try a change of tack. 'Tell us about the city,' I say. 'We haven't heard anything for three years. Are there people still alive? What are the police doing? The government?'

'Ah,' Gabriel says, 'that's a long story, my friend. First things first. I don't think you would be travelling such a distance without supplies. Go and get them. You can camp with us tonight.'

Again, the way he talks, half smiling all the time, how he's so comfortable and relaxed, puts me at ease. Kas nods. I volunteer to go because she has the rifle.

'Wils,' I say, 'come and give me a hand.'

When we get to the sacks Willow touches my arm. 'Finn,' she says, 'why did Kas lie about Rose?'

'We have to be careful, sus them out, decide whether we can trust them. Until then, the less they know, the better.'

Back at the fire, everyone is sitting where we left them. Rowdy has his head in Tahir's lap. Kas has the rifle on the ground beside her and her left arm stretched out to Gabriel. They're comparing tracking devices. I think of Rose stitching up the wound, where she'd gouged hers out, at my kitchen table on that day in Angowrie. It's months ago now but I still remember the smell of her, the way she bit her lip when she pushed the needle through, how it made me sick watching her.

Willow and I get comfortable, leaning back against the sacks.

'Tell us about the city,' Kas says.

'We were held in a processing centre on the outskirts,' Gabriel begins. 'Most of what went on in the city we only heard about second-hand or when we were transported out to the factories. Some of the drivers were kind. They spoke to us, told us what was happening.'

'The factories?' I ask.

'Abattoirs,' he says.

I think of the way he used the knife to cut the 'roo meat off the bone.

'The summer was hot, in between the thunderstorms. We were in crowded cells with no air-con. Each day more guards got sick or fled the city. Then the drivers stopped coming, too.

In the end, there were only half a dozen guards for a hundred of us. They climbed into a truck one afternoon and drove out, leaving the gates open. We knew nothing of how to survive in this land. Most of us had come on boats, separated from our families. We thought we were the lucky ones.'

'What do you mean?' I ask.

Tahir takes up the story. 'You heard about them turning boats back?'

I remember this; it was on the news a lot.

'That was in the early days, when there was at least some concern for our safety. But boats were getting through, so then they...'

He turns away.

'They started sinking them,' Gabriel says. 'They shot at them. Blew them up.'

Kas stares into the fire. 'That's so fucked up,' she says.

I can't look at her.

'What happened when you escaped from the processing centre?' I ask, changing the subject.

'Everyone split up. Some took their chances going into the city, some decided to stay at the centre where there was shelter. But Tahir and I started walking, west. Always west.'

'You've walked two hundred kilometres,' I say.

'Yes, it was a long journey. There were many travellers on the road but the virus was spreading faster than we could walk. People became sick, falling along the way. More No-landers joined us. We didn't want to admit it but we must have had some immunity to the virus. And the work in the factories had made us strong, so we were able to keep going when others couldn't.'

'Did you pass through Wentworth?' I ask. It seems like a lifetime ago that I caught the bus to school there.

'We couldn't avoid it,' Gabriel continues. 'It was a very dangerous place but there was food there so we stayed for most of the year. We did things that we are not proud of, just to eat, just to survive.'

'We've all done things we're not proud of,' Kas says.

'By the autumn things began to change. The army—or what was left of it—took control of Wentworth. There was talk of a council being formed. Some power was restored—we had electricity for one hour every third night.'

Kas and I look at each other, hardly able to believe what we're hearing.

But Gabriel shakes his head. 'Don't get your hopes up. The virus was still active and there were too few people to help.'

'And,' Tahir continues, 'that meant No-landers, Sileys, were needed to do the work. To be slaves once more.'

Gabriel cuts in. 'We set out west again. There weren't as many people on the road as the previous year, but there were gangs of men who demanded food in exchange for safe passage. We never trusted them. But we met other No-landers along the way, all of us fleeing into country we didn't know.'

'Some people must have helped you,' I say.

'Some, yes. They gave us a little food if we promised to keep moving. Eventually, there were fifteen of us, too many to rely on the charity of others. So we—'

'Gabriel!' Tahir interrupts, shaking his head.

'You can't have done anything worse than we have,' Kas says.

'You don't want to know,' Tahir replies.

Everyone is quiet, then. The fire crackles and hisses—the wood is too damp to burn properly. Willow has nestled her head into my lap and I can feel her breathing long and slow. The night envelops us, with only a sliver of moonlight visible through the trees. We can feel the cold at our backs and hear the movement of the wind in the forest around us.

'We need to sleep,' Kas says. 'But I think we should take turns to keep watch.' She picks up the rifle again and lays it across her knees. 'I'll go first,' she says.

Gabriel and Tahir don't seem to care about having a sentry. They back away from the fire and pull a couple of blankets out of a bag. I've woken Willow and grabbed our sleeping bags from the sacks.

'Wake me when you get tired,' I say to Kas.

I scout around for a large, dry branch to throw on the fire before lying down on the opposite side to Tahir and Gabriel. Willow snuggles next to me and I drift off as the flames take hold of the dry wood.

7

Sometime during the night, Kas shakes me and I wake with a start.

'What's up? I ask.

'Nothing. I'm tired—I need you to take the watch.'

It's the first chance we've had to talk privately since we came across Tahir and Gabriel. I take her arm and we move away from the fire.

'Do you trust them?' I say.

'I dunno,' she says, knowing immediately what I'm talking about.

I like the way we are starting to think the same way.

'Something doesn't add up, them looking for Rose, giving us the rifle. Why? It doesn't make sense,' I say.

'There's no guarantee they're telling us everything, either,' Kas says. 'Sounds like they've been through some tough times, though.'

We both turn back towards the fire.

'You know how to use that?' she asks, looking at the rifle

'Vague idea.'

'Be careful, then. It's loaded and ready to shoot.' She leans into me. 'I'm so tired,' she says.

'Hey,' I say, as she turns back towards the fire. 'Where did you learn to use a rifle? Rose said Stan never let you two near them.'

'Tell you in the morning,' she says, lying down next to the fire and pulling the sleeping bag over her.

The moon is higher now and its dim light filters through the trees. The wind shifts in the higher branches, but even though the air's cold, it's nothing like the winter. There's a stillness about the forest at night that I love, as though everything has slowed down at the end of the day.

I climb a few metres up the side of the cutting and choose a spot with some bracken to sit on and a tree to lean against. The rifle feels strange in my hands, the wood grain worn and shiny. Dad was so anti-guns. He hated them. Now, though, they could be the difference between living and dying. If we could take this with us to the valley, we would have a big advantage over Ramage's men, if they're still there. But having a gun is one thing; having ammunition is another.

It's hard to tell how deep we are into the night but the stiffness in my back and hips keeps me from dropping off. The fire is dying down and I can just make out the four shapes lying around it.

I feel a gentle tap of a boot on my leg and wake to see Kas standing above me. The first light of morning is inching its way through the trees.

'Hey, soldier,' she says. 'You know what the penalty is for falling asleep on your watch?'

I climb to my feet and realise she has the rifle in her hands.

'Sorry,' I say.

'Sorry's not good enough, it's the firing squad for you.' It's light enough for me to see the flash of her teeth when she smiles.

'Come here,' she says. 'I'll give you a quick lesson.'

She walks a little way into the bush. 'This is the bolt,' she says, pulling the metal lever up and back. 'This checks to see if it's loaded and each time you shoot you do it again to reload. Brace your shoulder and be prepared for the kickback.'

'Where did you learn all this?' I ask.

'Stan. He never let Beth or Rose know, but he taught me when we were out working in the paddocks.'

'But when the Wilders came to your farm, Rose shot Rat, not you.'

'Lucky shot. She had no idea what she was doing.'

I hear the sound of a branch breaking and the murmur of voices. We walk back to find Willow, Tahir and Gabriel standing around the fire. There is a haunch of kangaroo in the coals and the air is filled with the smell of singed fur. Gabriel picks it up by the bone sticking out the end and flicks it over. Both the No-landers look at the rifle Kas is holding.

'Have you decided what you are going to do?' Tahir asks.

'We're going north,' Kas says, holding their gaze. 'When we've taken Willow home we'll bring Warda to you.'

Gabriel and Tahir talk quietly for a minute. The rifle is important in what happens now—who's holding it and who wants it.

'It's a good offer,' I say. 'Warda's a warrior, she's exactly the sort of leader you need.'

'How do we know we can trust you?' Tahir says, his eyes narrowing. In the daylight, tattoos are visible on his neck. There's hardness in his voice.

This is like watching a game of chess, waiting for the first false move.

'Actually,' Kas comes back at him, 'I don't think you've got a choice. We're going north regardless of what you do. You can go and search the coast as long as you like but you won't find Warda. You'll only get hungry and tired, maybe get captured by Wilders.'

'We still have to trust that you'll bring her to us.'

'Why wouldn't we? Safety in numbers. We could all work the farm together.'

The other thing I'm learning about Kas is that she's a great liar. She does it without having to stop and think and she eyeballs them as she talks. It makes me wonder whether she's always told the truth to me. Somehow I doubt it.

'Do we have an agreement?' she says.

Gabriel and Tahir must have met some tough people when they escaped the city but they can't quite figure Kas out.

'Do we?' she says again.

Tahir can't bring himself to say he agrees, but he nods, short and sharp. Gabriel looks relieved.

'Good,' Kas says, reaching her hand across the fire. Tahir takes it but he holds her there a little longer than I'm comfortable with, maybe making the point that he's stronger than her; she's got the better of him this time but that doesn't mean she always will.

'And what will you two do?' Kas asks.

Again, Tahir takes the lead. 'We will return to our farm and tell the others that we have found the girl with the mark on her face and that she has promised to bring her sister to us. That if she does not arrive before the full moon, we will hunt her down.' The whole time he speaks he keeps his eyes locked on Kas. I see her birthmark flush slightly.

'We'll bring Warda by the end of the month,' she says. 'You have my word.'

'But,' Tahir says, 'I have no way of knowing if your word is worth anything at all.'

Over a breakfast of meat and canned beans, we trade information about the country to the north. Kas warns them to stay clear of the Monahans. Gabriel gives very specific directions to their farm—north-west of Swan's Marsh, in the foothills of the main range. A creek passes through their paddocks on its way to the Barton River, downstream from Longley. There is an old fire tower high on the ridge overlooking the farm, which makes it easier to find, as long as you know what you are looking for. They use the tower as a lookout; it gives a clear view all the way out to the river.

The sun is fully up by now and we pack up the camp quickly. Gabriel and Tahir will travel with us as far as Pinchgut, where we'll turn east along the logging track.

The road is a mess, and the remaining snow is thicker on the ground. The storms must've been fierce up here.

It takes us most of the morning just to get to the approach to Pinchgut. It looks completely different from the last time we were here. We almost miss the logging track. It's here we say goodbye to Tahir and Gabriel.

Tahir rummages in his bag. 'You'll need these,' he says, holding out a small box. 'Bullets. Try not to use too many.'

'Thanks,' Kas says. 'See you on the full moon.'

He nods, turns on his heels and follows Gabriel up towards the cutting at Pinchgut.

'Hey,' I call after him. 'I don't suppose you heard anything about an older guy; his name's Ray? Might have been captured by the Wilders—taken back to Longley?'

Tahir doesn't turn around.

'No,' he calls over his shoulder.

~

We follow the track for half an hour before stopping to rest. Kas throws her sack on the ground and slips the rifle off her shoulder. Just having the gun with us changes how we travel. We can defend ourselves if we're attacked, rather than relying on running and hiding. Willow's carrying the bow and arrows. They might be useful when we get to the valley.

I can't stop thinking about Wentworth—that the army was there. They even had electricity. 'Things could be changing, Kas. For the better.'

'I'm not sure I believe everything they said. No one tells the truth anymore.'

'Like you, you mean?'

She thinks about this for a while. 'What I told them was a version of the truth,' she says, looking off into the bush at the side of the track.

'We might need their help, Kas. We've got more in common with them than with anyone else,' I say.

'I have,' she says. 'But I'm not so sure about you. Harry and Stella, they're more your people.'

Willow pipes up at the mention of her parents. 'You could come and live with us, Finn.'

The idea of splitting up hadn't even occurred to me.

'My home's on the coast,' I say, a little stronger than I intend. 'Always has been, always will be.'

Kas opens her sack and takes out some of the strips of kangaroo meat Gabriel gave us before we left. They still have the charcoal on the outside but once we scrape it off the meat is delicious. I'm okay with not talking for a while. The conversation was going somewhere I hadn't anticipated and I need time to think through what might happen after the valley.

I watch the way Kas eats, her eyes constantly roaming, wary the whole time. Before we left Angowrie, I thought I was getting to know her again, but since Ray's place she seems distant. We're making decisions together at the moment and I want it to stay that way.

The track is tough going but the further we follow it the less damage has been done to the forest. The snow has almost disappeared. Still, it takes us most of the day to reach the logging coup. We decide to spend the night there. It's safe to have a bigger fire; even if someone saw the smoke they'd take days to find us. We have more kangaroo and beans for dinner and Rowdy loves the bones.

I find my way through the bush at the bottom of the coup to the stream where Kas climbed the rock slab with Yogi. It was a trickle when we were last here but now water gushes over the rocks. I haven't washed since we left Angowrie, so I strip off and ease into the water. I dance about like a madman, splashing myself and washing as best I can. I'm about to climb out when I see Kas standing above me.

'You look like a skinned rat,' she says, sitting down on the rocks and pulling her knees up to her chest.

'Where's Willow?' I say.

'She's okay. Rowdy's with her.'

'It's bloody cold in here.'

I keep dancing around, trying to stop myself freezing to death.

Kas stands up and turns her back, pulls off her clothes and soon we're both jumping up and down like idiots, laughing and screaming in the cold water.

'You didn't tell me it was this cold!' she says, climbing out.

We both collapse on the warm rocks, lying on our stomachs, close enough for our shoulders to touch.

She sees me looking, reaches across and puts her hand over my eyes. 'Come on,' she says. 'Willow'll be wondering where we are.'

I wish we could stay here a little longer, soaking up the last of the sun. It feels wrong to be putting our manky old clothes back on and pulling dirty shoes over clean feet.

Kas leads the way as we climb the rock slab.

When we reach the track up the side of the coup, she takes my hand. I keep looking at her, trying to match her with the girl that killed two Wilders a couple of days ago, the one that bartered a deal with the No-landers. I'm glad she's on my side.

Tonight the twilight lingers as we find a protected spot to roll out the sleeping bags. All I can think of is Kas lying on the rock shelf, her skin against mine.

Kas's body is so different, now. She's thin but that just high-lights her muscles. I've noticed, too, the way she protects the side of her face where the birthmark is. She'll always sit on my left, so it's on the opposite side. But I don't see it anymore. I just see her. Her eyes and her mouth and the way her breasts push against her shirt. I lean over, wanting to touch her face, and she smiles.

The darkness of the bush closes in on us and I drift off to

the sounds of some animal rustling around in the long grass, probably a fox or a possum looking for an easy feed. I feel safe—no one's expecting us to be out here, no one's on the lookout for us.

8

There's been a dewfall overnight and the sleeping bags are damp. The three of us walk down to the pool to wash and have a drink. We eat the last of the meat while the sleeping bags dry in the sun. It's tempting to stay here longer, to sit on the grass and doze for a while, let the world wait. Kas feels it too. She squats behind Willow and braids her hair. It's a half-arsed job, though—Willow's hair is so thick and tangled already. Eventually, we pack up the sacks and begin the climb down the rock shelves on the north side of the ridge. Once we hit the bush again we turn east along the base of the cliffs. It feels strange, retracing our steps, like a little bit of our history rewinding. I've got no idea what we'll do when we get to the valley but Willow is moving more quickly now, smiling at the thought of home.

There's a real difference travelling with food in your stomach and plenty of water. We don't feel as driven to keep moving. Plus, we're not being chased this time. It's tough going on the wet, soggy ground but once we get out of the first gully and start moving parallel to the ridgeline, the ground dries out. We want to stay as high as we can, for the shelter of the cliffs and for the view to the north. We'll need to get a glimpse of the open paddocks in the valley to know when to start making our way down.

Kas moves ahead of me and Willow, dropping back every now and again to check on us, then striding off on her own again. She looks at home here, moving easily through the bush.

We take a break after an hour or so, when we find an opening in the canopy that lets more sunlight through.

'We should make it to the valley before dark,' I say.

Kas has put the rifle on the ground next to her. She uses a twig to clean dirt from under her nails.

'We have to work out what we're going to do when we get there,' she says.

'It's a bit hard to say, until we find out what's happened since we left. We've got to expect the worst. I can't see Ramage giving up the valley now that he's found it.'

'But he left to get Hope,' Kas says.

'Yeah, but most likely he's got some of his men in the valley. He could've gone back there with Hope, but my guess is he headed to Longley for the winter. It would've taken too long to make it through to the valley with the weather turning and a baby to look after. And that woman with him at Ray's was a Monahan, so they would probably have gone to Swan's Marsh on the way.'

Willow has been listening intently. 'I just want Mum and Dad to be safe.'

'Me too, Wils,' I say.

It takes the rest of the day to come within sight of the valley. At first we get glimpses of the open paddocks, a different shade of green to the forest. The afternoon is growing cooler and mist is dropping off the higher ridges.

We choose a rocky outcrop above where the fences meet the bush. I don't want Rowdy giving away our position so I tap him on the head, and he drops. The three of us creep to the top and lie down. Willow has been quiet since the valley first came into view. I can't imagine what she must be feeling, not knowing whether her parents are alive or dead.

All the houses are still standing and, as best we can tell, the sheds too. This is a relief after what we saw at Ray's. There is smoke rising from the chimneys of two of the houses.

'We've got two choices,' I say. 'Wait for it to get dark and then go down and sus things out or stay put for the night and watch from here tomorrow.'

'We've come this far. I'm not sure I can wait till morning to find out what's happened.' Kas says, shooting a glance at Willow, whose eyes haven't moved from Harry and

Stella's house, her home.

'What about you, Wils?' Kas says.

Before the winter I couldn't have imagined us including Willow in any of our decisions, but now she's one of us.

'I want to see Mum and Dad,' she says.

Kas puts her arm around Willow's shoulder and talks quietly. 'You know they might not be there. They might've been taken somewhere else.'

'You mean taken prisoner?' There's the smallest quiver in her voice.

'It's possible, yeah. Ramage could've...' Kas's voice trails off. She squeezes Willow's shoulder.

Something grabs my attention. Movement in the valley. About a dozen figures have emerged from behind a stand of trees near the riverbank. We're too far away to make them out but there's something unusual about the way they're walking—in single file. If they're returning from the fields at the end of the day, they'd be walking side by side, talking about the work they'd done or what they'd be doing tomorrow. There's something else that's odd too—they're walking so close together they look as though they're connected in some way. But the last person is a good distance back holding something, like a hoe or a spade.

Or a rifle.

By the time the group approaches the buildings they're less than a hundred metres from us.

It's Harry I pick first, the way he walks, his back straight and his head high. He's at the front and now we can see the chains running from one man to the next.

Willow has recognised him, too. I grab her by the arm. She tries to wrestle free. 'It's Dad,' she says, her voice loud. 'It's Dad!'

I have to put my hand over her mouth and pull her into me. 'I know. I know, Wils, but we have to be careful.' I look her in the face as I say this and slowly take my hand from her mouth. She nods and then climbs back up to the top of the rock to watch what's happening.

Kas, who hasn't moved from her position, says, 'They're prisoners.'

Willow lies on her belly and buries her face in her hands.

Judging by their height and clothes, all the ones we can see are men. They disappear behind Harry's house and when they come into view again, a second guard has joined them. They shuffle up the ramp, with the man at the back prodding them forward with the rifle. They are unshackled one by one and pushed through the door, which is locked behind them.

When the guard turns, it strikes me how big he is. He looks taller than the height of door. He's huge.

We slide down the rock and sit with our backs to it. Rowdy senses something is wrong. He nuzzles Willow, who puts her arms around him and hugs him close.

'I guess we should have expected it,' Kas says.

Willow lets go of Rowdy and sits up, wanting to be included in the conversation.

Kas leans against the rock with her arms crossed. 'This changes things,' she says. 'Maybe we should backtrack and head towards Longley.' She stares at the ground while she talks.

'What if Hope's down there? What if they brought her here?' I ask. 'And what about Harry and Stella? And Wils, what's she going to do?'

'We came here to see if it was safe to leave her. Wils will have to come with us. There's no point her getting captured too.'

'Stop talking like I'm not here,' Willow says, standing up and putting herself in front of Kas.

I look around us. We're not far from the spot where Stella pushed Willow into my arms, pleading with me to take her away. I remember the look on Kas's face then too, angry and sympathetic at the same time.

'Finn,' Willow says. 'Make her stay. Make her help us.'

'I can't *make* her do anything, Wils. She has to decide for herself.'

Kas shoots me a glance like I've betrayed her in some way.

'Shit, Finn!' she says, 'I wish just for once you'd make a decision with your head instead of your heart.'

I can't help myself. I shoot back, 'I wish just for once *you'd* think of someone else. I know you've had a tough time and you never deserved any of it but you're not the centre of the universe.'

'Stop it!' Willow says, standing between us.

Kas drops her head, and I feel like a prick for what I said.

'Sorry,' I say, finally, unable to meet her eye.

Kas doesn't say anything and Willow sidles up to her. Kas drops her face into Willow's hair and kisses the top of her head.

'Wils, the peacemaker,' she says.

'We need to eat,' I say.

Darkness falls and we eat in silence. Willow sits between us but Kas and I steal glances at each other. It's our first real argument.

'All right,' Kas says.

'All right, what?' I say.

'All right, let's go down and check out the valley. See what's going on. We're *just* checking it out though, not doing anything stupid.'

'Okay.' I let this sit for bit. I don't want her changing her mind.

A smile creeps across Willow's face.

'I don't think we all need to go, though. We don't know what we'll find. I think I should go on my own first,' I say.

I expect Kas to argue but she agrees right away. 'I'll wait here with Wils and Rowdy. If there's any trouble, give us the bird call. And here,' she says, holding the rifle out to me, 'take this.'

'Nope. I can move better without it. And if I get caught, at least you'll have it.'

Again, she doesn't argue. Willow is sticking close to me.

'Don't worry, Wils. I'll find them,' I say.

She hugs me. 'Be careful,' she says, her voice muffled against my jumper.

I turn to go but Kas grabs my arm. 'Don't be a hero, okay,' she says.

I can't take a chance on moving in the open, so I walk along the fence until I'm above the cluster of sheds behind the houses.

The shearing shed is the closest but I can't get to it without crossing about fifty metres of paddock. I slide through the lower strands of wire and start my dash for the cover of the buildings. But I'm only halfway down the hill when a herd of cows appear out of the dark. They spook immediately, bellowing and taking off towards the shed. Worst of all, they have bells around their necks! Suddenly the valley is filled with the sound of their clanging.

Shit, shit, shit!

The door of the nearest house, Harry's place, flies open and I see two figures on the porch, both with rifles. One darts back inside and comes out with a lamp. Then they open a gate and walk up the hill towards me. The cows have settled a bit and are ambling towards the sheep yards in the corner of the paddock. I hide myself as best I can among the herd, moving with them.

The two men are no more than ten metres away. Luckily, the lamp doesn't throw much light. If they had a torch with a beam, they'd spot me straightaway.

'You see anythin'?' one says.

'Can't see a f-fuckin' thing. P-probably one of them w-wild dogs Fenton saw l-last week.'

'Could be.' He sounds unconvinced. 'Don't reckon it'd have a go at a cow, though. Sheep maybe.'

'Well, th-they've s-settled now. And it's c-cold out here.' He turns and starts to walk back towards the house.

The other one has the lamp. He steps closer and the cows fidget and move. He holds the lamp higher and lifts his head to peer into the dark. He's not just looking, though; he's listening. I'm pressed up against the side of one of the cows, holding my breath.

Finally he lowers the lamp and turns back towards the house.

'Better let Rat know, I s'pose,' he calls to the other man, who's already at the gate.

Rat is here! I can't believe what I'm hearing. If Rat's here, maybe Ramage is too.

I wait until the door closes before I walk slowly and carefully to the sheep yard fence. There's a maze of small pens and gates that lead to the back of the shearing shed. The sliding door we saw the prisoners pushed through is off to the left, at the top of a wooden ramp. It's too exposed, so I make my way through the yards until I can crawl under the shed, which is half a metre off the ground. The flooring is solid but I guess that the holding pens inside the shed will have slats.

I know when I reach the right spot because the sheep shit is piled knee high. Fortunately it's pretty dry. I find a place where I can sit and lean against a steel support.

There are voices above where I'm sitting. My problem is I don't know whether there are guards in the shed or not. It's not likely with the locked door but I can't be sure.

There's a rusty squeak above my head as a door opens. Heavy boots take a couple of steps onto the slats and, before I realise what's happening, piss starts streaming down onto my leg. I roll to the side but my foot catches on a loose piece of barbed wire. The pissing stops but the boots above my head don't move. I hear the zipping of a fly but no movement for at least a minute. I'm frozen to the spot, holding my breath. The barbed wire has cut my ankle and blood trickles into my boot.

The slats creak as the man lowers himself onto his hands and knees.

'Is someone there?' he whispers.

My body is shaking. I consider sitting up, removing the loop of wire and getting out of here. Running.

'I can see your leg,' the voice says. 'Who are you?'

Time seems to stall then. I'm too scared to say anything, to move, to breathe.

'Please,' the voice says. 'Wait. Wait.'

The slats creak again as he gets to his feet and opens the door. He stops and I hear him whisper a little louder, 'Harry. Come 'ere.'

Harry!

Someone else treads carefully into the pen and drops to his knees. A familiar voice says, 'Who's there?'

'Harry.' My voice is so low I can hardly hear the words myself. 'It's me, Finn.'

'Finn! What the—?'

I hardly know where to begin, what to say to him.

'What's going on, Harry? What's happened here?'

'Finn,' he says again, and I can hear the disbelief in his voice. 'Ah, mate, it's good to hear your voice. Is Willow okay?'

'She's fine, Harry. She's safe.'

I hear something that might be a sob, or a quick intake of breath.

'What about you, Harry. Are you all right?'

'I'm alive but things are pretty crook. Have been since the day you left.'

'What happened?'

'We're prisoners in our own valley. Ramage went after you with half a dozen of his men, but I'm guessing you know that already?'

'Yeah. We made it back to Angowrie, though.'

'Good for you. Is that where Willow is?'

I consider telling him she's here but for the time being it might be safer for him not to know his daughter's only a few hundred metres away.

'Yeah,' I say. 'What happened here after we left?'

'Ramage's men overpowered us. They run the valley now. We work the fields with armed guards watching us every minute of the day. Then they lock us up at night.'

'And Ramage?'

'He hasn't been back. Haven't seen him all winter.'

There's so much I need to tell him, but there's no time now.

'What can we do, Harry?'

'We?'

'Kas is here. Waiting up in the bush.'

He takes a while to consider this. 'Who's with Willow then?'

'Don't worry, she's safe. Trust me.'

He considers this for a few seconds, then says, 'There are six of them, Ramage's men. They're all armed. Living in our houses and sleeping in our beds.' The words spit from his mouth.

'And Stella?' I have to ask.

'They keep the women and girls separate.'

'What can we do, Harry?' I ask again. The door is opening and closing. More people are crowding into the pen. There's a murmuring of voices.

'Best we can tell, they've got all our weapons. They knew where to find them.' He pauses. 'It's Tusker. He turned against us. He's working with them.'

'Where's Tusker? Is he in your house?'

'No, that's Smale and Douglas. Tusker's gone. Left just before the winter set in. There's another bloke in charge. Fenton—he's a man-mountain—and violent.'

The murmuring rises again. 'Bastard!' I hear someone say before Harry shushes them. 'You can't mistake him, tallest bloke I've ever seen. Must be close on seven feet,' he says.

This would be the man I saw locking them in when they got back. 'We've got a rifle. And ammunition,' I say.

Everything goes quiet above me.

'They're dangerous, Finn. And Fenton's not the worst of them. Ramage's son is here.'

'Rat,' I say.

'You know him? He's as bad as Ramage. Worse in some respects. He'll kill you without a second thought.'

'I can't stick around here too long, Harry. Tell me what they do during the day. What's their schedule?'

'They wake us early. Feed us whatever shit they have left over then chain us together to head out to work. We work sun-up to sundown. No food during the day. Usually, four of them will guard us out in the paddocks.'

'So there's seven all together? With Fenton?'

'Yeah, Fenton's in charge of the work party.'

'So there are three left here during the day?'

'They guard the women while they work. Rat and two others.'

'What should we do?'

His voice is weary. 'Run. Get away from here. Go back home. Look after Willow for us.' The others have gone quiet.

'And if we decide not to? What then?'

'I'm serious, Finn.'

'So am I. We've dealt with Wilders before. We killed two of them down on the coast.'

'Don't think we don't appreciate you coming, but it's too dangerous. You'll just get captured, too. Or worse.'

'I'll chance it.'

Half a dozen voices all talk over the top of each other until Harry shushes them again.

His voice is different, now. Uncertain. 'You'll have to signal us in some way, let us know what you're doing.'

'You know what a wattlebird call sounds like?'

'Yeah.'

'That's my signal. Three calls, a couple of seconds apart. I'll wait till the work party is almost back.'

'We'll be chained. Not much use to you.'

'Who carries the key?'

'Fenton.'

'I watched you coming back this arvo. You only had the one guard.'

'Two go out to the valley entrance for the night and the

third one stays to clear up, put all the tools away. He's usually half an hour behind us.'

I'm trying to take all this in to pass on to Kas. I can't even begin to think of a plan yet but the more info we have the better.

'Okay. Got it. I have to go now, Harry.' I've untangled the wire from around my ankle and I'm ready to crawl back out into the yard.

'Finn?' Harry's voice is deeper, softer. 'Be careful.'

'I will. Oh, and Harry?'

'What?'

'Tell that bloke not to piss on me the next time will you?'

There are muffled laughs above.

9

I take the long way back to Kas and Willow, avoiding the paddock with the cows. Everything Harry has told me is swirling around in my head.

I give the wattlebird call and Kas steps out onto the highest rock. The clouds have cleared and the moon gives me just enough light to navigate up through the scrub to our hiding spot.

'You took your time,' Kas says before I can get a word out.

'Did you see Dad and Mum? Are they all right?' Willow asks. She must have been sleeping. She rubs her eyes as I sit down with my back to the rock.

'I saw Harry. I spoke to him. Stella's here too but I didn't see her.'

Willow jumps to her feet, hardly able to contain herself.

'What was all the noise when you first went down there?' Kas asks.

I fill them in on the cows and my conversation with Harry. Willow's head slowly sinks to her chest but I don't see any reason to hide the facts from her. She has to know how dangerous it will be to try to help them.

'Shit!' Kas says.

'Shit!' Willow mimics her and I have to smile. It's the first time I've heard her swear.

'There's nothing we can do until tomorrow,' I say. 'We'll have to watch and see what Rat and the other two do with the women and girls. If we can overpower them somehow, we could surprise the others when they come back from the paddocks.'

The deeper into the night, the colder it gets. The rock holds some warmth from the day so we lie pressed up against its base. Rowdy has walked off and found himself a snug spot in the bracken ferns.

I sleep in fits and starts, waking when I hear noises and drifting off again when I realise it's the wind or the cry of a night bird. By dawn I feel as though I've hardly slept but I must've grabbed a few hours.

Something doesn't feel right. I sit up quickly. Kas rouses with my movement.

Willow's sleeping bag is empty. I look to the top of the rock, expecting to see her up there, surveying the valley. Nothing.

Kas is still drowsy but there's concern in her voice. 'She might have just gone for a piss. I'll check.'

She scouts the surrounding bush, whispering Willow's name as loud as she dares. I pick up Willow's sleeping bag. It's cold.

Kas walks back slowly and we both climb up onto the rock.

The valley is quiet. There's no movement around the houses yet, no smoke from the chimneys. The sun hits the tips of the western ridge and some of last night's mist sits on the paddocks. We both scan for a sign of Willow.

'She was so close, we should have expected it,' Kas says.

'Wils is pretty smart. She won't give herself away. My bet is she'll try to find Stella.'

'But if she does get caught, it won't take long for them to realise she wouldn't be here on her own.'

She's right. 'I reckon we wait until the men have headed off to the fields,' I say, 'then we go down and look for Willow. Stay out of sight. Maybe we can hold off on making our move until later in the afternoon.'

We look at each other then, knowing how dangerous it will be. There's a moment of stillness when the bush is quiet, the sun shafting through the treetops and the breeze wafting around us.

The shock of a bell ringing in the valley sends us scrambling to the top of the rock. Two men walk across the yard to the shearing shed. One unbolts the door and the other, armed with a rifle, disappears inside. A few minutes later he emerges with the farmers. The men shuffle in their chains, holding them off the ground with one hand and leaning their other hand on the man in front to keep from falling over. They make their way across the yard and out along the road that leads to the paddocks. In ten minutes they've disappeared from view, hidden by the willows lining the river. One guard follows immediately but the second stops and looks from building to building, then up in our direction. I could swear his gaze lingers on our position just a little longer than anywhere else, but eventually he turns and follows the others.

There's no sign of life around any of the houses, though we know there are still three Wilders down there. And Stella, and the other women and girls. And, now, Willow too.

'I don't think we can wait any longer,' Kas says. 'Willow's changed all that. We don't know what we're going to find down there but we've got to check it out.'

I have to tie Rowdy to a tree. He hates it and frets and pulls at the rope. 'Sorry, boy,' I say. 'I'll be back as soon as I can.' I open a can of sardines for him, and Kas and I share some beans.

We stow our gear in a deep crack at the base of the rocks. It's then I notice something missing.

'Willow's taken the bow and arrows,' I say.

'Let's hope she knows how to use them.'

I tell Kas about the way Willow has been practising through the winter.

'Seems a lot happened back in Angowrie I didn't know about.' She slings the rifle over her shoulder and we start the walk down towards the buildings.

We follow the same route I took last night, staying in the cover of the scrub as long as we can. The cows are still in the paddock behind Harry's place. We move further along the fence, past the sheep yards until we're about twenty metres from the hayshed. From here we make a quick dash across open ground, one at a time. Kas holds the rifle in front of her, like a soldier heading into battle.

A sheet of corrugated iron is loose in the wall. We ease it open and slip through. There's hardly any hay to be seen.

'They've gone through most of their feed,' Kas says, looking around the near-empty shed.

From here we have a clear view of the other houses. Smoke rises from the chimney of Harry and Stella's place.

'Someone's in that one,' I say, pointing.

'That's where we start, then,' Kas says.

Adrenaline is running through me. I'm getting used to feeling this way again, on edge, nervy. But today feels different. Today, we're the hunters instead of the hunted.

The ground is muddy behind the sheds and we struggle to keep our feet, but we make it to the back of the house without giving ourselves away. We press against the wall at either side of the back door. We can hear voices inside. Male voices. Kas signals for me to move along the back and round the corner of the house. She'll do the same on the other side.

By the time I get to the front, Kas is already in position, crouched behind an old chest to the left of the front door.

I expect things to move quickly but everything seems to slow down. If they're going to leave the house this morning, they're taking their time about it. My heart is pumping fast and my legs are cramping from crouching so long. I ease myself down against the wall and stretch my legs. The sun is shining directly into my face and its warmth helps keep me calm. I close my eyes and try to slow my breathing.

After an eternity, the bolt slides open on the front door and I hear the shuffle of boots. At least two lots of footsteps crunch on the gravel in front of the house. Then they stop.

'Rat wants us to have a look for that dog from last night,' one says. 'I'll check around the shearin' shed. You look for tracks up along the fence.'

'He c-could have a l-look himself. Lazy b-bastard. And how come he gets to s-spend so much t-time in the women's house?'

The other man snorts. 'Why'd you reckon?'

'Fuckin' b-boss's son.'

'Just the way it is, Dougie. We gotta—'

He stops mid-sentence and the whole valley seems to be waiting for him to go on. My heart is jumping in my chest again but I shift sideways and peek around the corner.

The two men, who must be Smale and Douglas, are only ten metres away. One of them is tall with raggedly chopped hair. He is pointing. 'See there,' he says, one hand grabbing the shoulder of the other man. 'Past the hayshed, the old tractor.'

'W-what about it?'

'Watch. I seen somethin' move.'

'You're s-seein' things, Smale. There's n-nothin' there.'

'Wait.'

The tractor is about thirty metres away. It's rusted to a burnt orange and its wheel rims have sunk into the ground. I've got a slightly different view from the two Wilders and I'm sure I can see something sticking out above the back tyre. I can't be sure but it could be the end of a bow.

Willow breaks cover and begins to run, crouching low, towards the furthest house. She's hidden from the Wilders' view by the tractor but as she gets closer to the house they spot her.

'There!' one shouts, beginning to run after her.

'Well, b-bugger me,' the other says, almost laughing. 'W-where did sh-she come from?'

Then he takes off, too.

Willow is fast. She disappears behind the house before they are halfway to the tractor.

Kas grabs me by the arm and hauls me to my feet. We can't risk running in the open, so we backtrack behind the hayshed.

'They don't have guns,' she says, her breath coming in short bursts. 'They must've left them in the house. This could be our chance.'

There's a pile of firewood stacked about twenty metres from the next house. We take up position behind it.

Smale and Douglas have separated and they circle the building from opposite directions.

'Rat,' Smale yells. 'We got something.'

The door opens slowly and Rat appears, hitching his pants and struggling to do up his belt. He wears a dirty grey singlet and he limps heavily.

'What's up? he says.

'Ya won't believe it! We seen a girl, a kid, hidin' behind the tractor. She ran over this way.'

'You sure? The girls are inside.'

'Positive. Little blondie, she was.'

A smile spreads across Rat's face. 'Little blondie? I reckon I know who that'll be.'

He limps back inside and we hear stifled screams and raised voices. Female voices. Then, one by one, they stagger out into the light, their arms lifted to shade their faces from the sun. There are four of them, two women and two girls. I hardly recognise Stella, though I'm sure it's her. Her hair has been hacked back to her scalp and her clothes hang loosely from her shoulders. The other woman must be Rachel. The two girls cling to her.

Rat has a short-barrelled rifle and he uses it to prod the women forward. He separates Stella from the others and points the gun at her.

'All right, kid,' he yells. 'I've got your mum. Come out or so-help-me-god I'll shoot her.'

Stella looks wildly around the yard. Her body is shaking uncontrollably but her voice is strong, '*Run, Willow. Run!*' Rat smashes the butt of the rifle into her stomach. She staggers, then falls to the ground. Rat is on top of her, jamming the barrels into her back.

'I won't tell you again, kid,' he yells. 'I'll kill ya mum. Right now.'

Kas has lifted herself up to the top of the woodpile. She points the rifle to the ground and carefully opens and closes the bolt. Her hands move slowly and sweat runs down the side of her face. She brings the rifle up and rests the barrel on the top of the stack.

There's a stillness that comes with tension, like waiting for a storm to break.

Willow steps out from behind a cypress tree beside the house. She holds the bow, an arrow pulled tight in the string.

Stella has pushed herself up onto her hands and knees. She sees her daughter, just a dozen metres away. Willow stands with one leg slightly in front of the other, her shoulders back, like I taught her.

'Mum,' she calls. 'Mum.'

'Wils. My baby.'

A leering smile crawls its way across Rat's face. 'Well, look at this, boys,' he says. 'Little girl lost comes home. Don't it melt ya heart?'

Smale and Douglas edge towards Willow.

'I don't know if you understand the laws of physics, girl,' Rat says, 'but your little play toy's no match for my gun. Now, put it down and I won't shoot ya mum.'

Willow is panicking, pointing the bow at Douglas, then Smale, then back towards Rat. I can't stand it, I begin to move but Kas pulls me back.

The men are getting closer to Willow.

Stella lifts her head and says, 'I'm okay, Wils. I'm okay.'

Willow begins to lower the bow, still holding the arrow tight in the string. Just when I think she's going to drop the bow she brings it back up, pauses for a second, and shoots at Rat.

Everything happens in a blur, then. The arrow hits Rat just below his right shoulder. He yelps in pain and drops the rifle. At the same time one of the Wilders lunges for Willow and I hear a sharp crack so close to my ear it deafens me. He drops to the ground.

Kas has shot him!

The other woman and the two girls look around, confused. Willow has reloaded the bow and holds the second man at bay. Rat continues to curse and scream. Stella has his rifle pointed at his head.

Kas steps out from one side of the woodpile with the rifle aimed and ready, and I step out the other side. Everyone is confused, looking at each other and trying to work out what happened.

Kas screams at the other Wilder. 'On your knees! Now!'

Willow runs to Stella, who holds Rat's rifle in one hand and hugs her daughter with the other.

Rat tries to get to his feet but falls back to the ground, his pain now turning to rage. '*Fuck!*' he says, again and again.

Stella looks up at Kas and me and shakes her head. 'Finn,' she says, tears streaming down her cheeks. 'Kas.'

I can't help myself. I walk to her and throw my arms around her. I can feel the bones through her clothes.

Kas motions the second Wilder to his feet. The shot one hasn't moved. 'Finn,' she says, 'get some baling twine from the hayshed. Anything you can find.' She pushes the Wilder over next to Rat and gets him to sit down.

I take off, relieved to be moving. There's heaps of twine so I choose a few good lengths and take them back.

Rat is sitting on his arse, one hand gripping the shaft embedded in his shoulder and the other bracing himself to stay upright.

Kas squats in front of him, with the rifle pointed at his chest. 'Remember me?' she snarls.

Rat tries to spit at her. His voice is low, pained. 'How could I forget that ugly face?' he manages to say.

But Kas smiles. 'We should've killed you when you came to our farm the first time. If Rose'd been a better shot, you'd be dead by now. Not just a useless cripple.'

Rat is panting for air. His hand claws the dirt.

'Warda, you mean. I heard what happened to her. Served her right. Bitch!' he says.

Kas moves so quickly Rat has no time to evade her. She brings the butt of the rifle crashing across his jaw. I hear the sound of bone cracking and see a couple of his teeth fly into the dirt. He collapses against the arrow, pushing it deeper into his flesh. He lies still.

The other Wilder cowers. I've tied his hands behind his back so he pushes his forehead into the gravel as he tries to get to his feet. Stella is next to him in an instant. She brings her boot down hard on his back and holds him there.

We are all left standing in the morning sun, staring at each other and trying to figure what to do next. Rachel and the two girls look from Kas to me and back again. There's wonder and fear in their eyes.

Stella runs her hand through the short hair on her scalp. She looks towards the river, shading her eyes with her hand. 'They'll have heard the gunshot,' she says. 'They're working out by the valley entrance but the noise will carry. It'll take them half an hour to get here.'

Willow hasn't said a word. Maybe it's the shock of shooting Rat, or the sight of her mother all skin and bone. Stella tries to scoop her up in her arms but she doesn't have the strength. She hugs her close and mouths *thank you* to Kas and me.

Rachel looks as sick as Stella. Her skin is a dull grey colour, her hair knotted and wild. 'We need to get organised,' she says.

We drag Rat and the dead Wilder inside the house. I can't tell whether Rat is alive or not. When I try to shift him he shows no sign of life. Thick blood oozes from the wound and his jaw juts out at an odd angle where Kas hit him with the rifle. I don't want to risk him waking up and giving us away, so I tie him up and find a rag to wedge between his remaining teeth as a gag.

Back outside, Kas nudges the other Wilder with her foot and he struggles to his feet.

'What's your name?' she asks.

'D-douglas,' he says.

'Don't waste your time with him,' Stella says, standing behind Kas. 'He's as dumb as a box of hammers. Does whatever he's told.'

'I was j-just followin' orders,' he says, pleading.

When I get close to him I see he's not as old as the others, maybe in his thirties. Rough stubble covers his chin but his hair is thin enough to see through to the scalp.

'Well, here's an order for you,' Kas says, 'Shut the f-fuck up!'

I almost laugh, but time is running ahead of us and we have to get ready. We push Douglas inside with Rat and tie him to a cast-iron stove. Before I can get the gag into his mouth he spits, 'You're in s-so much sh-shit now, boy, and you d-don't even know it.'

I want to say something smart, like Kas, but all I can think of is, 'We'll see about that.' It sounds lame and he knows it.

We decide that Harry and Stella's place will be the easiest to defend. It gives us a clear view down the valley. We make our way back there. Stella struggles to walk the few hundred metres, and Rachel has to support the girls.

Once we get them inside, I step back out onto the verandah with Kas.

'They're so weak,' I say. 'They're not going to be much help in a fight.'

'I know, but hopefully it won't come to that.'

'What'd you mean?'

'I think we should go out, you and me. Ambush them before they get here.'

'It's too late for that. They'll be on their way. They must've heard the shot.' I can't figure out whether I'm being practical or I'm just plain scared.

'Think about it, Finn. For all they know Douglas could have been shooting at that wild dog they were looking for.'

'It's a big risk.'

'No bigger than sitting here and waiting for them.'

'We've got cover here.'

Kas stares out along the road. She's a different person, now, so sure of herself. If I hadn't seen her hands shaking when she raised the rifle to the top of the wood stack, I'd swear she's actually enjoying this, her chance at revenge.

I duck back into the house. Stella is sitting at the kitchen table, Willow behind her, with her arms around her mother's neck. Rachel and the two girls, whose names I don't even know, are sitting on the lounge room floor.

Kas is right, we'll have to do this on our own.

10

There are two guns in the house. We've got Rat's rifle too—
that's four weapons, not counting Willow's bow.

Kas, Willow and I barricade the windows and back door
with furniture and make sure Rachel and Stella have ammunition. Then we close the front door behind us so they can bolt
and barricade that too.

How have I ended up here, armed and heading into a fight?

Everything around me is at odds with how I'm feeling.
Sunlight streams into the valley, pushing the clouds back
towards the ridges. The wildflowers are all out along the edge
of the road and the winter-sown crops are pushing rows of

green shoots up through the dark soil. But my head is buzzing and all the colours blur.

Kas has our rifle and I've got Rat's. It feels strange in my hands, lighter than I thought it would be. The barrel has been shortened and the wooden stock is smooth. It feels oddly comfortable to hold.

We make a run for the willow trees near the river. We have to cross about three hundred metres of open ground, but it's the only place that's close enough to the road for us to see anything coming. The ground is wet and spongy after the winter, and our boots are soon caked in mud, slowing our progress. Sweat runs down the inside of my shirt and it's not just the mud that's making my legs heavy. I'm out of breath by the time we make the trees. Their branches are bare so it's only the trunks that give us any cover. A little further along, the river cuts in closer to the tree line. We can drop down onto the bank and still get a good view of the road.

'How long d'you reckon it's been since the gunshot?' Kas asks.

'Half an hour, maybe longer.'

Her chest rises and falls slowly. She's so much calmer than me. She puts her hand on my arm and squeezes.

We sit for ages, watching the road. Maybe the others didn't hear the shot, after all. Maybe the wind was too loud in the trees or they were shouting at each other at just the right time. Either way, we start to relax. We might have to wait until they finish work for the day, at least another seven or eight hours.

Stupidly, we haven't been watching in the other direction, back towards the buildings. When we do, we see Rowdy padding along, stopping every so often to sniff the breeze. He must have picked up our scent because now he slips through the fence and heads straight for us.

When he gets closer, I whistle and he picks up speed, his tongue lolling out the side of his mouth and his legs slipping a little in the mud. Finally, he reaches us and I try to pull him in to me. But he veers past us, his low growl turning into a bark. Kas and I spin around to see a man standing on the bank, a rifle pointed directly at us. He's huge. It must be Fenton.

Kas moves to lift her rifle but Fenton's voice comes low and hard, 'Go on, girl, pick it up. Give me an excuse to shoot you.'

He slides down the bank, holding his rifle steady and maintaining his aim. Rowdy's hackles are up and he bares his teeth.

'Keep that dog away from me or I'll shoot it,' he says.

I grab Rowdy by the scruff of his neck and drag him behind my legs.

'Actually,' Fenton says, 'I should be thanking the mongrel. I wouldn't have seen you two down here if it hadn't headed for you.'

He makes us sit on the ground against the bank then goes to kick our guns away. He stops when he sees the sawn-off barrel of Rat's rifle.

'You two better start talking,' he says. He crouches low, close enough for us to hear his nasally breathing. He looks much healthier than Stella and the others, well fed—his cheeks are red and rigger's gloves keep his hands warm. His hair is pulled into a ponytail. He half grimaces, half smiles, and his teeth are uneven under a thick moustache.

Kas has been quiet until now but she stares him in the face and says, 'We were bringing the kid back, Willow. We just wanted to leave her and go on our way.'

She's a good liar but Fenton shakes his head and he spits at her. The gob of phlegm catches in her hair.

'I know who you are, girl. That birthmark stands out like a beacon. And I know you're a fuckin' liar.'

He tells us to stand and turn around with our hands behind our backs, before pushing a piece of rope at me and telling me to tie Kas's wrists. Tight. He stays close, the rifle barrel an inch from my cheek.

Our plan has backfired before it even got started. I'm desperately trying to think of a way out.

Once I've tied Kas he shoves her to the ground and kneels on her back. Then he motions me in to him so he can tie my hands too. The rope bites into my wrists. I try to flex them so it will loosen when I relax but he directs a punch to my kidneys and I stagger forward. He drags me back by the rope and loops it around again.

When he's finished, he pulls us to our feet and starts marching us across the paddock towards the houses. He leaves two of the rifles, ours and Rat's, hidden under the bank.

As we walk, he talks. 'Dumb-arse kids! You're out of your league here, you should've known that.'

He laughs and prods Kas with the barrel of his gun.

'I'd keep you for myself if Ramage didn't want you so bad.'

Kas doesn't miss a beat. 'As if I'd let an arsehole like you anywhere near me.'

Suddenly Fenton is on top of Kas, his hand on the back of her head, driving her face into the mud. Her body writhes as she tries to get breath. But he holds her there, pushing his whole weight against her.

'Stop!' I yell, but he just looks up at me and smiles. I throw myself against him, but I bounce off. Kas is scrambling to get her face out of the dirt, spluttering and spitting, gasping for air.

Next thing, Rowdy goes at Fenton and grips his ankle just above the boot. Fenton howls, hopping back on one leg and trying to shake himself free. He raises the gun high then levels it at Rowdy.

The shot echoes around the valley and Rowdy slumps into the dirt. Kas and I kneel on the wet ground a couple of metres from him. I can't move.

Rowdy lies on his side, his breathing heavy, snuffling. He paws at the ground with one leg, trying to get to his feet. Blood trickles from his mouth and his eyes are wide.

Fenton stands over him, pointing the rifle at Rowdy's head. I throw myself forward, losing my grip in the mud, landing heavily on Rowdy. But I push myself up to my knees and lean in until I'm covering him.

My tears are mixed with snot and dirt and they land on Rowdy's coat. 'Don't!' I scream.

Fenton's boots move back in the mud. 'Get up,' he says.

I lean to the side and manage to get my feet under me, the whole time keeping myself between Fenton and Rowdy. Kas is dry retching, spitting dirt from her mouth.

'Now walk,' Fenton yells. He's backing away towards the road, his attention focused on the houses again. They'll have heard the shot.

Kas's face is covered with dirt and her hair is thick with mud. Her shirt is ripped at the back and her shoulder blades poke through. We trudge towards the road, Fenton behind us. When we reach the fence, we have to crawl under the lowest wire, rolling to the side to get to our feet again. Fenton just steps over it. I chance a look back at Rowdy but he hasn't moved. He's just a brown lump in a black field.

Fenton is limping, though, and his ankle is red with blood. Rowdy has bitten him deep. I'm past caring about my own survival, now. I turn and run straight at him, colliding with him front-on before he has time to lift the gun. He overbalances and I fall on top of him. Kas is beside me, kicking Fenton again and again. But he's so much bigger than us. He grabs Kas's leg and pulls it from underneath her. She falls heavily and I hear her head hit the ground. I've somehow managed to bite his neck and I taste the salty blood. But he throws me off easily and I land next to Kas.

Fenton climbs to his feet, picks up the rifle and stands above us.

'Stuff this. Who's goin' to know,' he says, pointing the gun at my head. I close my eyes. I try to think of Dad and Mum. My body shudders and I've pissed myself.

A shot rings out.

He must have missed. Then his whole weight falls over my

legs, the rifle caught between us. There's blood everywhere, but I can't tell whose it is.

I'm breathing. I'm alive!

There are other footsteps on the gravel now, coming closer. I wriggle and push and shove his body off me.

When I look up, Stella is standing on the road, blocking the sun. She has a rifle in her hands. I can't make sense of Fenton's face; there's blood all over it. His eyes are blank.

I feel a knife cut through the rope around my wrists. My vision is all blurred and I'm struggling to work out what's happened. Rachel is kneeling next to Kas, wiping the dirt from her face with her sleeve.

I stagger to my feet. My legs are like jelly, my pants wet with piss but I half walk, half fall down to the fence. I slide through the wire and run to Rowdy.

His body is warm and he's breathing. I lift him into my lap and push my face into his coat. Kas has followed and she kneels next me, running her hands over his body, searching for the wound. Rowdy's eyes stare at me, and he pants.

'Here,' she says.

She has her hand on the top of his back leg. Then she shifts her other hand underneath him.

'It's gone through!' she says, smiling and crying. 'It's gone through, Finn!'

She tears at her shirt and pulls away two strips, placing each one carefully on the wounds. Rowdy flinches and tries to get to his feet but I hold him tight. He licks my arm.

Stella calls from the road. 'We have to get back. The rest of them could be here any minute.' Rachel has picked up Fenton's rifle and she and Stella turn towards the house.

I lean over Rowdy and push my forehead against Kas's.

'Come on,' she says. 'We can carry him.'

I cradle Rowdy in my arms across the paddock to the fence, where I pass him to Kas. Between the two of us we get him to the house.

Willow runs at Kas and hugs her.

'What's happened to Rowdy?' she asks.

'He's hurt,' Kas says.

'Will he be okay?'

'I don't know.'

Kas and I take Rowdy to the washroom. The wound doesn't look quite as bad once we clean away the blood and caked dirt. He paws at us, as if trying to understand what's happened to him. When we're done, we wrap him in a blanket and bring him into the kitchen where it's warmer.

I notice how messy the house is. Dirty plates are stacked in the sink, clothes and food scraps litter the floor. Stella seems not to notice—all her attention is on Willow. She holds her as though she might disappear again at any moment.

We barricade the door and sit in the half-light, exhausted but knowing we'll need our energy again soon. I've seen two men, maybe three, die this morning. I know it was part of our plan, but I can't quite believe what's happened.

Stella sits across the table from me, still holding the rifle she used to shoot Fenton. It's the first time I've had the chance to look at her closely. Her face is lined in a way I don't remember last autumn. Her hands are scabbed and her nails black with dirt. Her collarbones stick out against her shirt and her chest is hollow.

She sees me looking and drops her head. 'It's been hard, Finn,' she says.

I don't know what to say.

'Did Harry tell you what happened after you escaped?' she says.

'A little.'

'As if it wasn't bad enough having Ramage's men ruling us night and day. But Tusker'—she spits his name out—'Tusker turned against us. He was as bad as them.'

Then her face brightens a bit. She reaches across and takes my hand. 'How is Rose? She would've had the baby by now.'

Kas sits down next to me. She leans her forehead against my shoulder. When she speaks I can feel the words on my skin.

'Rose died,' she says. 'And Ramage took the baby. We called her Hope.'

It sounds like too few words to explain all the pain and anger and hurt.

'I'm so sorry,' Stella says. I can tell she wants to ask more, but she looks at Kas, releases my hand and sits back in her chair. Through habit, she goes to run her fingers through her hair, smiling when she realises how silly it must look. 'I swear I'm going to sue that hairdresser,' she says.

Willow rubs the uneven fuzz on her mother's head. 'It feels like a rabbit,' she says.

Stella asks Rachel and the girls to come and sit with us. She introduces Rebecca and Katherine. Kas already knows them. She stayed with them when she was captive here last year.

Looking at the girls sitting side by side I realise they're twins—probably a year or two older than Willow. They have the strange combination of blue eyes and jet-black hair. Like Rachel and Stella, their faces are gaunt and there are dark rings under their eyes. They huddle close to each other, holding hands and hunching their shoulders. They haven't said a word.

Kas sees the hesitation in the women and girls. 'Right,' she says. 'We've got no way of knowing when the others will be back but we have to be prepared.'

I can see what Kas is trying to do—sound confident, take charge.

'Wils,' she says. 'You take the twins back up to the rock where we slept last night. All our gear is there, so make yourselves comfortable and stay out of sight.'

Willow looks to Stella, who nods.

'Surprise is our best defence,' Kas says to Rachel and Stella. 'We need to wait until they're in the yard before we make our move.'

I'm onto her plan now but I can see a problem. Fenton's body is still lying in the middle of the road. They'll see it before they get anywhere near the building.

'I'm going to shift Fenton's body,' I say. 'I'll stay hidden out there and get behind them when they've passed. Fenton left the rifles on the riverbank.'

Kas nods. 'What other guns do we have?'

'This one,' Stella says, lifting the rifle by her side. 'Rachel's got Fenton's and we found another one by the back door.'

'Good. Give me one, and you and Rachel stay in here with the other two. Barricade the doors again after we've left.'

Willow leads the twins out of the kitchen. Stella follows, and hugs her briefly. Willow passes the bow over her head and hitches the arrow bag onto her back. 'Don't worry Mum,' she says, 'I'll be okay.'

'Go now,' Kas says. 'Stay low and be careful.'

'I should move, too,' I say. 'I'll give you the whistle to warn you in case you can't see them coming.'

'I'm not staying in here,' Kas says. 'I'll be behind the old tractor. I want to be able to move if I have to.'

I look back. Stella is standing with the rifle cradled in her arms. She's got her shoulders back and her chin up. Suddenly, she looks ready for a fight. Rachel is next to her. I don't know anything about her, how reliable she might be, but we don't have any choice now. We need to believe in her, too.

Kas and I run for the protection of the low hedge by the front gate. Clouds have moved in, bringing a chill to the air. The wind is picking up and it's starting to rain.

It's all quiet out along the road and Fenton lies where we left him, about two hundred metres away.

Kas touches the side of my face with a cool hand. 'Good luck,' she says.

Then she pushes me away and I start running.

11

My legs feel like they've got lead weights in them. I'm pushing straight into the wind, and the rain needles my face.

Fenton lies on his back, the rain, heavier by the minute, pounding into his chest. Blood washes off his body and soaks into the gravel. I'm about to try moving him when I remember something Harry told me last night—Fenton has the keys to the chains. I slip my hands into his pockets, but they're empty. Maybe he left the keys with the others. Then I notice a chain around his neck. It's smeared with blood but when I pull it up, there are two keys on it.

Everything is wet and slippery now, making it hard to get

a grip on him. In the end, I sit down on the road and roll him with my feet. He's heavier than I could have imagined but, with a lot of swearing and kicking and pushing, I eventually roll him into the ditch at the side of the road. Then I pull clumps of weeds from the soft soil to cover his body.

My breath is coming fast again and I can't tell if it's cold or fear that's making my body shake. I slide through the fence and run flat-out for the willow trees, falling into the bank and hugging my knees to my chest when I make it.

I'm hidden from the road but open to the wind and rain. My clothes are saturated and I keep having to push the wet hair out of my eyes. I shimmy along to the overhang where Fenton hid the rifles and pull them out. Rat's is wet and caked in mud, so I leave it there. But ours is still pretty clean. I wipe it with my shirt and check the bolt.

I wonder what Mum and Dad would think of me, holding a rifle and preparing to shoot someone. Somehow, I've avoided killing anyone, so far. It's happened around me but it's been kind of surreal. Kas has killed three men and I'm alive because of it. I know it's changing her; she's done it to protect us and now I'm going to have to make a decision about doing the same.

The adrenaline has been keeping me awake but my stomach is growling for lack of food. I've had nothing to eat since the can of beans I shared with Kas hours ago.

It's well past midday when I hear movement along the road— the sound of metal dragging on gravel. Eventually they round a bend about fifty metres from where I'm sitting. There are eight men stretched across the road, chained together at the ankles. They're walking in a horseshoe shape, protecting three other men, who each carry a rifle.

The Wilders are using the farmers as a human shield.

Harry's in the middle of the line. He turns his head from side to side, scanning the valley and houses. He knows something's happened. I'm a good distance from them as they pass. I climb carefully over the bank, sliding the rifle in front of me, and press myself against the trunk of a big willow. I give the wattlebird calls—one, two, three. Harry turns in my direction and touches his ear. He's heard me.

I wait until they've gone past before I risk moving. I have to stay behind them, where the guards are exposed. They pass the spot where Fenton's body lies in the ditch. No one sees him.

There's a lot of open ground to cover to get to the road so I have to take a chance on none of the Wilders turning around. Thankfully, it's raining. It pounds onto the gravel and disguises any noise I'm making.

I get to the fence without being seen, but now they're a fair distance ahead of me on the road. Something is happening in the group—the horseshoe is closing in, getting tighter. The Wilders are making sure they're protected. They stop when they reach the main gate where the road opens out into the yard in front of the houses and sheds. I find some cover about twenty metres behind them where a crumbled stone wall meets the road.

'Fenton,' one of the Wilders shouts. 'What's goin' on? Come out.'

The yard is silent but for the steady fall of rain on the roofs of the houses.

'Fenton,' he calls again. 'Stop stuffin' around.'

I can't see Kas near the tractor. *Where is she?*

One of the Wilders raises a shotgun and shoots into the air. The farmers duck, hunching their shoulders against the noise.

'Anyone here better show themselves right now. And,' he yells, stepping forward and pressing the shotgun to the back of Harry's head, 'I mean right now.'

Seconds tick by. No one moves.

I try to push myself upright, pressing against the wall to stop my body shaking. I know it has to be me that makes the move. I've got the advantage; I can take them by surprise.

I punch my thighs to get them moving, hold the rifle high and step out onto the road.

I walk ten paces towards them, forcing myself to put one foot in front of the other.

When my voice comes it's cracked and jittery.

'Don't move,' I call.

The farmers drop to the ground, exposing the Wilders, who all swing around to look at me. I've got the rifle raised and I'm trying to keep it steady.

'And who are you?' the Wilder in the middle says.

Somehow, I keep moving forward, stopping a few paces from them.

'Didn't think this out too well, did ya kid?' the one with the shotgun says. 'You can only shoot one of us. Put your rifle down and we'll let you live.'

'Put yours down and I'll let *you* live.' It's Kas. She's standing in the yard, no more than ten metres away.

They swing around to her.

'She's not joking, Wilson.' Stella steps out from behind the hedge to their left, her gun raised as well.

The Wilders are confused, looking for a way out of the trap.

'Where's Fenton?' Wilson, the one with the shotgun, asks.

'Dead.' Stella says, her voice defiant.

'And Rat? Smale? Douglas?'

'Various levels of dead,' Kas calls.

All their attention is now on Stella and Kas. The farmers edge in, tightening the space around the Wilders. The man closest to me looks up and nods.

The other two Wilders lower their weapons but Wilson holds his high. I keep him in my sights, looking along the barrel and aiming for his back.

Suddenly he lurches towards Harry bringing the shotgun down towards his head.

Do it, Finn. Do it.

I squeeze the trigger. There are more shots. Stella and Kas must have fired at the same time. Wilson jerks one way then the other, before dropping heavily onto the road. At the same moment, the farmers push in and throw themselves onto the Wilders in a pile of swinging fists and boots and chains.

Finally, all the commotion dies down. The farmers pick themselves up, trying to manoeuvre the chains so they can stay on their feet. Harry has his foot on the back of one of the Wilders who looks to be unconscious. The other one is on his side, in a foetal position. Blood pools under his cheek.

Harry looks at me and smiles wearily.

I throw him the key and the men pass it around. As each frees his legs he steps away from the group and rubs his ankles. One picks up the shotgun and stands guard over the Wilders.

Stella throws herself at Harry. They hug, burying their faces in each other's shoulders.

After a while Harry holds her at arm's length, a smile mingling with his tears. 'I like what you've done with your hair,' he says. Stella laughs and softly punches him in the chest.

The rain has eased and, as if on cue, the sun breaks through. Harry and Stella look to me and open their arms. I drop the rifle and fall into them. It's so comforting after all the cold and fear of the day—the warmth of human bodies brought together. Stella motions to Kas, who hesitates, looking around and shifting her feet in the gravel.

'Come here,' Stella says, but Kas stays put. I take her hand. She pulls back but I draw her in, her body rocking and swaying until her resistance falls away. I hold her as tight as I can. Harry and Stella enclose us and we stand there in the sunlight, the tension seeping from our bodies.

It takes most of the afternoon for everyone to come to terms with the new situation. I recognise Simmo, from the meeting last autumn. He and Rachel walk everywhere hand in hand.

The dust has barely settled when Harry spots three small figures running through the top paddock, scattering the cows and making their bells ring out across the valley. Rachel, Simmo, Stella and Harry walk as quickly as their tired bodies can carry them to the gate to meet Willow and the girls. Willow throws herself at Harry and Stella, nearly knocking them over and the twins fall into the arms of Rachel and Simmo.

The two Wilders in the work party, Dillon and Ricardo, are taken to the shearing shed and their wounds tended to before they're locked inside. Douglas is marched over to join them. Simmo tells us Rat is dead and three of the men dig graves close to the bush in the paddock above the hayshed. There's no ceremony—Rat, Fenton, Smale and Wilson are buried quickly, with nothing left to mark their graves. I want no part of this. I don't want to see their bodies or watch as they're covered with soil. But I have a burning question that I need answered.

One of the men on burial duty is Jack, who was with Harry and Tusker when they first caught me at Pinchgut Junction. He looks ten years older. When I saw him last he was wiry and strong but now he's half-starved, like everyone else. He walks back from the graves, a shovel over his shoulder, looking exhausted from the digging.

'You come to piss on me?' he says, smiling.

'What?'

'That was me in the shearing shed last night. You scared the shit out of me!'

'Sorry,' I say, only half meaning it.

'You did good, Finn.'

'There's something I need to know,' I say, unable to look him in the eyes. 'Was it me who...'

'You want to know if you killed Wilson?'

'Yeah.'

'I don't think so. He had a wound to his arm, but a bullet hit him in front. That's what killed him.'

'Thanks,' I say, unsure of how I feel about the news.

When we've walked back to the sheds, he puts his hand on my shoulder. 'Don't dwell on it, son. It's over.'

Harry decides they'll kill one of the cows and we'll have a feast. The afternoon is spent cleaning out the houses. Any of the Wilders' gear that's not useful is piled up in the yard and burned. Stella and Harry pull the rugs up off the floor and air them in the afternoon sun. Then they scrub and clean everything, wiping away the stench of the men who've been living at their house. By evening, it looks as neat as it did when I first saw it. Willow cleans her own room, dragging dirty blankets outside and hanging them over the fences.

Stella looks at her, shaking her head in disbelief.

'What have you done to my little girl, Finn?' she asks, smiling.

'She can hunt and shoot and fish as good as me,' I say. 'Skins a rabbit quick and clean, too.'

Willow pretends not hear our conversation but she walks a little bit taller, her shoulders back. I wonder how she feels about having shot Rat with the arrow this morning, whether it's playing on her mind. She doesn't show it if it is.

Kas spends the afternoon tending Rowdy. She's made a bed for him on the floor of the washroom and cleaned the wounds again. Stella has given her some antiseptic cream for him. He's breathing more easily and he lifts his head to drink. We won't know how serious the damage is until he starts to heal and tries to walk. But that will be a while yet.

The slaughtering of the cow takes place behind the shearing shed. I've seen enough blood for one day, so I leave that job to the others. By evening they've rigged up a spit across the coals of the fire in the yard. Great chunks of meat are skewered and we take it in turns to rotate them over the coals. Fat drops into the fire and the smell brings everyone out.

There are four other farmers: three men—Steb, Vic and Sam—and a girl named Kate, who'd been kept separate from the other women. She looks healthier but I wonder what price she's paid.

Kas brings a boy over to meet me. James is the one who led her to the valley last autumn. He looks about thirteen or fourteen years old, scrawny, with a face full of pimples. He hides behind a mop of ginger hair, unable to look either of us in the eye.

'They call me Bluey,' he mumbles, shifting his bare feet in the dirt.

'Course they do,' I say, smiling.

Kas is confused. 'Why?' she asks.

'He's got red hair.'

'So much stuff I'm never going to understand,' she says.

When the meat is cut up and everyone has a full plate, Harry says grace. 'Lord, thank you for delivering us from slavery. And thank you for Kas and Finn and for bringing Willow home safely.'

'Amen,' everyone replies in harmony. Except Kas, who looks down at her food and gently shakes her head.

Chairs have been brought out from the houses and a long table set up. There are potatoes and pumpkin cooked in the coals and someone has found some lettuce and dandelion leaves for a rough salad. I barely remember the taste of meat like this, but my mind reels back to Saturday-night dinners when Mum would cook a roast. We were always careful to cut the fat off each slice but now I can't wait to taste its crispy, charcoal flavour. The conversation falls away as we all eat. Every now and again someone burps or farts and everyone laughs, but mostly all I can hear is the chewing of meat and scraping of knives on plates.

I've brought Rowdy out and put him on a blanket next to my chair. He can smell the meat and every instinct must be telling him to eat, but he lies with his face resting on his front paws. I try him with a small piece but he just licks it.

Almost everyone goes back for seconds—and thirds—until we are all so full we can hardly move.

There's a feeling of spring in the evening air. It's crisp but not biting like the winter nights have been. A crescent moon rises over the ridge to the east. It draws the attention of everyone at the table, their eyes lifting to the night sky as they think about living freely in the valley again. The first stars begin to show themselves.

Jack breaks the silence. 'What now, Harry? What about Ramage? The winter might've kept him in Longley but he'll be back before too long.'

'Tonight's not the time to be making decisions,' Harry says. 'We're all tired and it'll take us a while to get back on our feet. But we can't leave it too long. We need to prepare to defend the valley. And we have to get more crops in the ground as soon as we can.'

I look around the table and see the mix of concern and exhaustion on every face. Me, Kas and Willow are the fittest of all of them, even though we've had a tough winter ourselves. But at least everyone has a full belly and they'll be able to sleep in their own beds tonight.

For a while I sit next to Harry and he tells me what it was like being held prisoner. 'They had no idea about farming,' he says. 'Lazy bunch of bastards.'

There's something I want to ask him. 'Where did all the weapons come from, Harry? When Ramage and his men came looking for Rose in Angowrie all they had were sticks and knives. Now they've got rifles.'

'Fenton bragged about it all winter. They found a bloke holed up out past Simpson. He was a doomsdayer, planning for the end of the world. Turns out he wasn't far wrong. Anyway, he had enough weapons to fight a small war. That's where they got them. They'll run out of ammo eventually but for now it makes them more dangerous than ever. At least we've got some of their rifles, though I dunno if that's a good thing or not.'

Steb, Vic and Sam volunteer to guard the valley entrance for the night. They walk off into the dark with rifles over their shoulders and a couple of small bags of leftover meat. Everybody else drifts off to their homes until it's just Kas and me left sitting in the warm glow of the fire.

'You okay? she asks.

All afternoon I've been trying not to think about what happened. I've kept myself busy because I'm afraid of feeling the metal of Fenton's gun pressing on the back of my head again. 'I thought I was going to die.'

'But you didn't,' she whispers.

'I was scared shitless.'

'We all were.'

'You didn't show it. How do you do that?'

Kas stares into the coals. 'I don't know.' She bunches her hair in her hands and pulls it back off her face. 'Something broke inside me when Rose died. I've got nothing to lose.'

'You've got me to lose.'

'You know what I think?' she says.

'What?'

'I'm not made for happiness. Even when it's all around me I don't know how to be part of it.'

'I've seen you happy.'

'When?'

'At the rock pools, that day with Willow.'

She thinks about this. 'It didn't last did it? That was the day before Rose died.'

'Just because something bad happens doesn't mean that's it forever.'

'Bad things have been happening all my life.'

I'm not sure I have an answer to that. For all the shit that's happened to me in the last three winters, I had thirteen years of love, of being normal. Kas never had any of that.

'It's okay,' she says. 'It's the way it is; the way I am.'

'But you can change.'

'Yeah. Maybe. Right now though, I'm so tired.'

She stands and holds her hand out to me. This is the confusing bit—she keeps pushing me away, but here she is reaching out again.

Inside the house she opens the door to Willow's room, then turns to look at me. 'Goodnight,' she whispers.

Lying on my bed, my body aches for sleep but my mind is racing. Today was tough, but if we stick to our plans there's only going to be more of the same. It's so real now, different from sitting at the kitchen table at home and talking about it happening some time in the future. The future is now and it scares me to death.

12

Out in the kitchen there's a clatter of plates and cutlery—the sounds of a family getting started on the day. I stumble out to find Harry, Willow and Kas sitting at the table and Stella standing at the stove with a steaming pile of pancakes.

'They're pretty basic, just flour and water and a couple of eggs, but they'll fill us up,' Stella says. She brings the plate to the table and we all link hands. Even Kas joins in.

'Lord, bless this food and keep us from privation,' Harry says.

We are about to start on the pancakes when Willow says, 'Wait!' She jumps out of her seat, opens one of the kitchen cupboards, sticks her head in, rummages about and emerges holding a jar.

'Remember when we made plum jam last year?' she says to Stella. 'I hid this one for when we ran out.'

We barely talk as we hoe in.

After we've played rock, paper, scissors for the last one, we sit back and enjoy the satisfaction of a full stomach. It's a rare feeling.

'There's a meeting this morning in the community hall, if you want to come,' Harry says, looking to Kas and me. 'You'll have a say, I promise you.'

'No fights?' I ask Harry, trying to keep the smile from my face.

'No fights,' he says.

'What about ear-biting?'

Kas punches me hard on the arm. 'Smart-arse,' she says.

The meeting room looks different from last time. All the windows are open and the space is flooded with light. The chairs are still in the same arrangement, with an inner and outer circle. The first thing we do is move them to form one big circle.

Slowly, everyone emerges from the other houses and the room fills. Steb sits down and tells us Vic and Sam will stay out at the valley entrance until they're relieved by the next watch. Simmo and Rachel walk through the door, holding hands. Jack enters on his own and sits next to Simmo.

Harry begins with a short prayer, and then gets straight

to the point. 'We have to discuss what we do from here. We know we have to be prepared to defend the valley when the time comes but we need to regain our strength after the winter before we can hope to win any sort of fight. For the time being, Ramage has no way of knowing what's happened. We need to make sure it stays that way.'

Simmo's voice is deep, considered. 'We have to keep the prisoners here, make sure they don't escape,' he says.

'I don't like imprisoning anyone,' Harry says, 'but we've got no choice.'

'They had no qualms about imprisoning us,' Rachel says.

Harry thinks for few seconds before replying. 'As much as I hate what they did to us, those three were just following orders. Ramage calls the shots.'

Kas has been sitting quietly, shifting her feet on the wooden floor. 'How much do you reckon they know about Longley, about who's been coming and going from there?' she says.

'Dillon and Ricardo have been here since the first day the Wilders appeared in the valley but Douglas arrived later, just before the winter set in properly. It's a fair bet he came from Longley,' Harry says.

'Why is that important?' Rachel asks.

Kas looks around the circle and I know she's trying to work out how much to tell them.

Stella reaches over and touches Kas's arm. 'It's okay,' she says. 'You can trust us. Whatever you want to do, we'll support you.'

Kas is still uncertain so I decide to speak up. 'You all know Ramage has Rose's baby. We're going to find her and bring her home. We promised Rose before she died.'

I can hear the intake of breath around the room.

'You mean you're going to Longley?' Simmo says, shaking his head. 'That's suicide, Finn. Stupid talk. You were lucky these last couple of days. You had the element of surprise on your side. I'm glad you came, but don't kid yourself you're any match for Ramage. He's got twenty men back in Longley, maybe more by now. You won't stand a chance.'

'I know you think it's stupid, all of you,' I say, looking around the circle again, 'but we're going anyway, Kas and me. You can help us or not. It's up to you.'

Stella doesn't hesitate. 'Tell us what you need,' she says.

'We need to talk to Douglas.'

'Harry?' Stella says. He and Jack stride out of the room. While they're gone Kas shifts a little closer to me.

Douglas looks like a scared animal. His hands are tied behind his back and his eyes dart around the room. Harry and Jack walk either side of him, almost lifting him off the ground with their grip on his arms. They pull an empty chair into the middle of the circle and push him into it. He cowers like he's expecting to be hit.

Harry sits next to us and says, 'Tell us the truth, Douglas, and I promise no harm will come to you.'

He nods but he's shit-scared.

'Were you in Longley at the start of the winter?' Harry begins.

'Y-yeah,' he says.

'Ramage was there?'

'I s-seen him a couple of t-times, yeah.'

'You know about the baby he brought back with him?'

Kas sits forward, straining to hear Douglas. His voice is nervous and whiny.

'Everyone knew about the b-baby. F-fuckin' thing never stopped c-crying.'

Kas is on her feet. Harry holds his hand up to her and nods. 'It's okay,' he says.

But Kas can't contain herself. 'Where's the baby, now?' she demands. 'Where's Hope?'

Douglas's lip curls up and he snarls, 'W-wouldn't you l-like to know?'

Kas is ready to leap at him; I can feel it. I pull her back into her chair.

But Jack reacts as well. He squats in front of Douglas, grabs him by his shirt and pulls him in close. 'You need to think about something, you dumb prick. Yesterday I buried four of your mates. And you know what I felt when I shovelled the dirt onto their shitty bodies?' He leaves the sentence hanging.

Douglas's whole body shakes.

'Nothing,' Jack says. 'That's what I felt. So if you think I'll hesitate to dig another hole next to them, think again. Now,' he says straightening Douglas in his chair, 'Kas asked you a question and if you don't answer it I'm going to get my spade and start digging.'

'B-but you said...' he pleads to Harry.

'I said, if you tell the truth, you won't be harmed.'

Douglas shrinks in front of us. All the defiance leaves his body and he starts to whimper.

Jack's in his face again. 'Should I get my spade, then?'

'N-no,' Douglas mumbles. He wipes his nose with his shirt, leaving a trail of snot on the sleeve. 'A f-few days before I left,' he says, 'the b-baby disappeared from the f-feedstore. The M-monahan woman, Bridget, sh-she took it.'

Kas is on her feet again, pacing up and down in front of him. 'You mean she stole her?'

'N-no. Ramage. He t-told her to t-take it.'

'Take her where?' Kas says.

'I d-dunno. He never said.'

'Swan's Marsh?'

'I d-dunno. Maybe.'

As Douglas is marched out of the room, I pull him aside. He cocks his chin at me and curls his lip but Robbo stands behind him and wrenches an arm up his back until he squeals.

'Did you hear anything about a raiding party down on the coast, maybe before winter?' I ask. 'A friend's house was burnt down. His name was Ray.'

'I h-heard n-nothin' about that. N-no one t-turned up at L-longley, that's for sure.'

Stella, Harry, Willow, Kas and I walk back to the house. The sun shines brightly and white pollen, like little threads of cotton, drifts through on the wind.

Inside, we sit down and help ourselves to leftover meat from last night.

'You reckon Douglas is telling the truth about Hope?' I ask.

'He's a Wilder: couldn't lie straight in bed,' Harry says.

Kas pushes her plate away. 'We have to go to Swan's Marsh and see if Hope's there. It kinda makes sense, Bridget Monahan looking after her.'

'But would he let Hope out of his sight?' Stella asks.

'Who knows,' Kas says. 'Douglas said Bridget and Hope disappeared. Ramage would've kept them close if he wanted them in Longley.'

Stella is watching Kas closely. Something is ticking over in her brain; I can see it. 'Suppose,' she says, 'suppose you were able to find Hope and steal her back. How old would she be now, three months?'

'Closer to four,' I say.

'So,' Stella continues, choosing her words carefully, 'how are you two going to look after a four-month-old?'

It's something that's been eating at me since Kas told me about her plan, way back before the winter. What do babies that young even eat? How would we keep her healthy?

But Kas sees where Stella's going with this. 'We'd work it out, wouldn't we, Finn,' she says, defiant and looking to me for support.

But I want to hear Stella out. 'What are you thinking?' I ask.

'Bring her here,' she says. 'Let us look after her. You could stay too if you wanted. Become part of the community.'

A crooked smile crosses Kas's lips. 'I'm a Siley, remember, and Hope will be one, too.'

Stella reaches across the table and tries to take Kas's arm, but

Kas pulls it away and squeezes her hands between her knees.

'You're not a Siley to us, Kas. You and Hope would be safe here,' Stella says. 'She would grow up surrounded by people who care for her.'

Kas squeezes her hands tighter. I'm sure she sees the sense in Stella's plan but it means letting go of control again.

'Think of the baby, Kas,' Stella pleads, her hands still reaching across the table.

Kas doesn't respond. She gets up and heads out the front door. Stella goes to follow her but Harry holds her back.

'You go, Finn,' he says.

I don't know what more I can say to change Kas's mind. I do think Stella's plan is a good one, but there's no way I'm going to stay in the valley. I'm heading back to Angowrie when all this is over and I want Kas to come with me.

I find her sitting on the little stone wall outside the gates of the main yard. Her legs dangle over the side and she swings them back and forth, her heels hitting the wall. I pull myself up beside her.

'I know,' she says.

'You know what?'

'That Stella's idea is a smart one. It'd be best for Hope.'

'Why didn't you tell her that?'

'Because then I'd have to make a decision.'

'About?'

We're close enough for me to see the deep brown against the white in her eyes.

'About staying here or going back to Angowrie with you.'

'We're a long way off that decision,' I say. 'We haven't even found her yet. We don't know exactly where she is, don't know how we'll get her away from Ramage. Let's work that out first.'

'Could you stay here, though?' she asks. 'If we got Hope back, could you stay here with us?'

'I...'

'It's okay,' she says, but I can hear the hurt in her voice. 'Everything you have is back on the coast.'

'Not just everything I have. Everything I *had*. It's home to me. It's where Dad's buried. It's where I feel the most like...'

'Like what?'

'Like me, I guess.'

13

The next morning, Kas and I hardly talk to each other. She doesn't look at me over breakfast and then she heads out to the paddocks with Stella and Willow. She's avoiding me. In the afternoon we work together, sorting seed potatoes in the shed, cutting them into halves and quarters ready to plant. Harry and Jack work alongside us. When I try to catch Kas's eye, she looks away.

'What's up with you two?' Jack asks, his knife working away without him having to look.

'Nothing. We're good, aren't we Kas?' I say, trying to lighten the mood.

'Yeah, course we are,' Kas says, but her voice sounds strained.

The rest of the day is taken up with checking on stock and how much grain is left for planting. Harry reckons the paddocks are in good shape because the farmers have all been forced to work them through the winter. It was Ramage's plan to have them provide food for his men in Longley.

The working day is cut short by exhaustion. After sunset, I find Harry sitting on the cross rail of the cattle yards behind the house. His big frame, wasted from hunger and hard work, seems lost in his clothes. I climb up next to him and we both look out towards the top paddock and the ridge that rises above the far end of the valley.

'You and Kas, you've been through a lot together,' he says. He rubs the palms of his hands together then slides his wedding ring up and down his finger.

'Yeah, we have. We're pretty close.'

'So are you...?'

'What?'

'Sorry, Finn, it's none of my business but you haven't had a parent round for a while so if there's anything you want to ask me, don't hesitate.'

'Thanks, Harry, but I reckon I'm good.'

He sits his hands flat on his thighs then, like I've seen him do in the meetings. 'So, are you having sex?'

I blush. It's not the sort of stuff I've ever talked to anyone about, but my curiosity gets the better of me. 'Nah. It's not that I don't want to, but I'm never really sure where I stand with her.'

It's easier not to look at him as I talk. I make as though I'm really interested in the grass below the fence.

'It's going to take time for her to trust anyone,' he says. 'She's had a whole life of people taking advantage of her.'

'But she knows I'm not going to.'

'*You* know you're not going to, but it doesn't mean she knows it.'

I hadn't thought about it from her side.

'What more've I got to do?'

'Be patient,' he says. 'She'll come around. Keep doing what you're doing—show her you care, look out for her.'

'I reckon she does more looking out for me,' I say, thinking of the last couple of days.

'There you are, then. You're looking out for each other.'

The back door of the house opens and Willow calls us in for dinner. As we walk towards the porch, Harry puts his hand on my shoulder. 'Any time you want to talk, Finn, I'm here,' he says.

The next few days pass quickly. The nightly meetings are taken up with preparations to defend the valley. In the meantime Kas and I gather as much information as we can about what to expect when we leave. There's a coolness between us that feels awkward. She doesn't say anything, but I know she's thinking about what'll happen if we make it back to the valley with Hope.

We've decided to go the quickest way, via the plains, rather than trying to get back to Pinchgut. Harry tells us about the railway line that runs next to the highway as it heads west towards Longley. It'll be dangerous country to travel through but we'll only need to make our way about twenty kilometres before we swing south, back towards the main range and Swan's Marsh. We'll check there first, in case Douglas is telling the truth and Bridget Monahan has been entrusted with Hope.

Food is running low so the farmers decide to harvest some of the winter crops early. This means some extra food to take with us. We've made no decision about when we'll leave, but the time is getting close.

Late storms delay us, pushing through the valley, with sheeting rain that fills the river until it breaks its banks. Everyone welcomes the rain, even though it means working in mud up to our ankles. We know it will keep Ramage in Longley a little longer and give the farmers more time to regain their strength.

The three prisoners are forced to work alongside everyone else. They whine and complain their way through each day but no one gives them any sympathy. Jack threatens to shoot them if they don't shut up and get on with their work. Me and Kas are treated as equals, given our share of food and encouraged to take part in community meetings. Slowly I see Kas dropping her guard, becoming less suspicious of them. And I notice the way the younger men, Vic and Sam, look at her. They sidle up to her during breaks in the sowing, chatting with her while they eat their lunch. But each time, she moves near to me and we look like a couple, even if I don't feel like we are.

Another week passes and we know we have to leave. Rowdy is improving by the day but there's no way he'll be able to come with us. Willow takes over caring for him and she promises she'll have him fully healed by the time we come back. Whenever that might be.

Harry has a plan to deal with Ramage. It makes sense. 'Sooner or later,' he says at the next meeting, 'Ramage'll come with his men but we don't know when. I've talked with Jack about this and I reckon we should let one of the prisoners escape. Allow him to get back to Longley and tell Ramage what's happened.'

Conversations break out around the room but Harry shushes them. 'Think about it,' he says. 'If we can lure Ramage here, we can be prepared for him. Capture him or'—he hesitates—'kill him. It also buys some time for Finn and Kas to find Hope.'

Jack speaks up. 'I'll guide Kas and Finn as far as Swan's Marsh. From there, they're on their own.'

'So, who do we allow to escape? And how?' Rachel asks.

'Of the three of them, Douglas is the most stupid. I doubt he'd see through it. We could take him out on a work detail close to the valley entrance, make it look as though we're not watching and let him take off. He won't hesitate if he gets the opportunity,' Jack says. 'We'll give him a few hours head start, then I could set out with Finn and Kas.'

Everyone is looking from one person to another in the circle, weighing up the plan.

Finally, Simmo says, 'It's not ideal and it could stuff up if Douglas doesn't make it back to Longley, but it might just work.'

'Ramage will have his raiding parties out on the plains as soon as the weather eases,' Jack says, 'so Douglas will only need to find one of them. From there, we have to rely on Ramage being a vengeful bastard and I reckon that's a safe bet.'

All of this talk has been going on around us but now Harry asks Kas and me what we think.

'I agree with Simmo,' Kas says.

'Yeah, me too,' I say. 'And thanks for taking the risk for us.'

Kas nods in agreement.

Kas and I leave the meeting anxious but excited. We'll be on our way soon. Neither of us is looking forward to travelling into Wilder country but there's something that burns deeper than the fear of getting caught—the promise we made to Rose, to bring Hope home.

The weather begins to ease again. We get a couple of sunny, dry days and the river drops a little. Everyone has been forbidden to speak about the plan for fear of the prisoners picking up on it. Kas and I have packed and we're ready to go. We're getting edgy now.

Harry and Jack are waiting on the porch one morning. Jack has a small pack on his back and he carries a rifle.

'Vic and Steb have headed out to the valley entrance with Douglas. Today's the day. Be ready in an hour,' Jack says.

Kas and I grab our things. Stella has baked some bread with the last of the flour. I don't want to take it but she insists.

'You're going to need every bit of strength you can muster,' she says.

When we are just about ready, we go in to see Rowdy. He knows something is up. He tries to get to his feet but I soothe him with a scratch under the chin.

A knock comes at the door and Jack calls, 'It's time.'

Stella stands in the kitchen, one hand on the table, the other rubbing the fuzz on her scalp. 'You two come home safe. Promise me.' She hugs us, one then the other. She holds Kas a little longer, kissing her on the top of her head. 'And look after each other,' she says.

I go to shake Harry's hand but he's having none of that. He wraps his big arms around me and holds me tight.

Willow stands back by the washroom door, looking at her feet and biting her lip. Kas squats down in front of her. 'Hey, fighter,' she says, 'you keep everyone safe here, won't you?' Willow nods, still unable to look at Kas.

Finally, Willow runs across the room and throws herself at me, burying her face into my chest. She pulls me down and whispers in my ear, 'I love you, Finn.'

'Keep practising every day with that bow,' I say. 'Remember, shoulders back, right arm high—'

'And breathe,' she says.

The rest of the community has gathered in the yard to see us off. Simmo shakes my hand and wishes us luck, while the twins gravitate to Kas. Jack is already at the gate, giving us the hurry-up.

'You bring that baby home safe, now,' Rachel says.

14

The sun has some sting in it by the time we go through the gates and begin the walk out along the track. Jack reminds me a bit of Ray—the way he used to walk, with short strides on bowed legs—though Ray always seemed closer to the ground. My heart burns in my chest when I think of Ray and the way he must have died. I wish I'd been there to help him. After all he'd done for me, I should have checked on him during the winter. I owed him that much.

After about an hour's walking, the valley starts to narrow. The willows thicken along the river and the ridges on either side press in closer. Ahead of us, there's a wall of dense bush, gums and acacias. The track is blocked by two huge fallen trees but Jack leads us down closer to the river where a rocky path winds its way through the undergrowth for a couple of hundred metres. Finally, the bush starts to thin and we get glimpses of sky and plain.

Jack stops and gives a whistle. An answer echoes through the bush. We hear movement in the scrub and Steb and Vic appear, with big smiles on their faces.

'Did he take the bait?' Jack asks.

'Course he did,' Steb says, laughing. 'Took off straightaway; couldn't believe his luck.'

'How far did you track him?'

'Till he hit open country. Couple of ks. He knew which way to go. Like a rat up a drainpipe, I reckon.'

'We'd best not stuff around then, eh?' Jack says. 'Stay close. It gets tricky from here.'

There're no formalities with the men. Jack leads us off and Vic and Steb melt back into bush. Within a few minutes we're pushing through chest-high bracken and scattered stringybarks. We don't appear to be following any track but Jack doesn't hesitate, pushing diagonally downhill now, veering west. Soon we have a clear view of the plain, broken only by stands of cypress trees that shelter the remains of farmhouses.

When we reach the beginning of the open country, Jack stops and we sit for a while. It's good to get the weight of the packs off our backs. My shirt is wet with sweat and Kas's hair is plastered to the side of her face.

'You need to get your bearings,' Jack says. 'You'll have to

find your way back on your own.'

Kas and I look at the way we've come, both thinking the same thing—*how will we ever find the valley again?*

'Out there,' Jack says, pointing towards the plain. 'You see the closest windmill, the one with tanks next to it?'

'Yeah,' I say.

'Now look a k further north. There's another windmill. No tank. Just the windmill. See it?'

'Yeah, I see it.'

'When you're coming back this way, walking east, keep an eye on the two windmills. When they line up, that's when you turn into the trees, head uphill. That marks the valley entrance.'

The plain is crisscrossed with what must once have been fences. There's no movement out there other than the wind rippling through the long grass, which is a rich green after the winter rains. The Barton River snakes its way across the plain, marked by the red gums that line its banks. Closer to us, powerlines show the old highway and, parallel to it, the raised bank of the railway.

We rest back on our packs now, enjoying the warm sun. I pull out Stella's loaf of bread and break off small portions for each of us.

'You'll need to make that last,' Jack says, refusing the piece I offer him. He stares out across the plain as though he expects to see something out there, or someone.

'Have you always lived in the valley, Jack?' I ask.

He takes a deep breath and busies himself untying and retying his bootlaces. 'No,' he says.

We wait.

'I farmed out near Freshwater Creek, north-east of here. My wife and I, we had three kids. Tim, he was the oldest, twelve when the virus came. Then Maisy and Noah. Ten and seven.'

'Did they...?

'All of them. My wife, Belle, she went first, then the little ones. I thought Timmy was going to be okay. We survived as best we could but then the people came from the city, from Wentworth, from all over. The Sileys among them brought the second wave of the virus. It was worse than the first. Timmy died within a couple of weeks.'

I shoot a look at Kas. She shakes her head. The whole time Jack's speaking he doesn't look at us once, just stares at the ground, talking in short sentences.

'I headed west. Found the valley by chance. Took to the hills to avoid the raiding parties, the gangs. Couldn't believe my luck. The community took me in.'

'I'm sorry,' I say.

'It's okay, son. It's been shit all over. Everyone's been affected one way or another. You're no different from me.'

Kas flinches, but she doesn't say anything.

Jack's on his feet, keen to get moving again. 'We've got a solid day's walk ahead of us until we turn away south again. Keep your eyes open. This weather'll be bringing the Wilders out.'

The walking isn't too hard; we're moving mostly through bracken and stands of manna gum. We cross half a dozen small creeks, all flowing strongly after the rain. They give us the chance to refill our water bottles and splash ourselves to cool down.

By nightfall, we're still walking parallel to the highway. We've seen no one all afternoon but as the light falls away we pick up the glow of fires, three of them at intervals across the plain.

'They're on the move,' Jack says. 'I dunno how far north Ramage controls but he'll use this spring and summer to expand his territory. Pity help anyone out there.'

We can't risk a fire. We've pushed a few hundred metres back into the trees and found a sheltered spot by a creek. We eat some dried meat and a little more of the bread, then collect armfuls of bracken to make ourselves comfortable. Jack moves off on his own while me and Kas hollow out a space to sleep. It's cold. The wind has picked up and roars through the higher branches of the trees. We snuggle down, huddling together for warmth. I lie behind her with my arm around her, moulding my body to hers. She rests her hand on mine.

I haven't slept in the open for while, not since we travelled to the valley from Angowrie. It's uncomfortable after the bed at Harry and Stella's but eventually exhaustion gets the better of me and I drift off to sleep.

I've forgotten how noisy the bush can be in the morning. The wind's dropped and the screeching of cockatoos and the laughter of kookaburras fills the air.

We pack quickly, have a bite of bread and meat, then we're off again. Jack has said nothing since last night. He motions us to follow him back down to the tree line. When we reach it, we turn west again, moving at a good pace, Jack in front, Kas in the middle, then me. I like walking behind her, watching her strong legs under the weight of her pack.

I almost walk into the back of her when she stops suddenly. Jack has one hand in the air and the other pressed to his lips. We drop down for cover. I haven't seen or heard anything but Jack has his ear lifted to the breeze. We slide our packs off and crawl forward. A fallen tree gives us some protection closer to the open paddocks. We hunch in behind it, listening.

There are voices. Close.

Jack inches his way up to look over the log, and Kas and I follow.

There are three of them. Wilders. They're standing above someone lying on the ground, someone curled up in a ball, protecting themself. The Wilders are laughing.

A voice rises above the noise of the bush—a girl's voice, high pitched and angry. 'Bastards,' she screams. 'Bastards.'

Kas crawls back and grabs her rifle. She doesn't hesitate, even when Jack tries to grab her and pull her down. She moves fast, keeping herself hidden until she's within a few metres of them. Jack has picked up his rifle and hands me mine. We jump the log and hurry after her.

Before we can get to her, Kas steps out and shows herself, her rifle raised to her shoulder and pointed at the Wilders.

'Leave her alone,' she says though gritted teeth.

The Wilders are startled. They back away, looking at Kas then at each other.

'Well, look at this,' one of them says. A crooked smile shows nothing but black gums. But his eyes widen when Jack and me step out of the bush behind her.

'You got them covered?' Kas asks.

'Yep.'

She kneels down beside the girl and gently touches her shoulder. The girl looks up, her body uncurling.

'Are you okay?' Kas says.

The girl braces herself on her hands as she tries to stand up. Kas helps her to her feet. It's hard to tell how old she is. Her face is bruised and swollen. She has a cut above her right eye and blood trickles down her cheek. Her clothes, or what's left of them, are torn. She does her best to hitch her dress onto her hips and pull the frayed straps over her shoulders. She's shorter than Kas, and her skin is a lighter brown. Her hair is pitch black and straight, her arms and legs thin and, strangely, she wears a pair of green sneakers.

'She's ours,' one of the Wilders says.

'Yours?' Jack asks. 'Or Ramage's?'

The three of them look like all the other Wilders I've seen, hair long and matted, clothes dirty but warm, and solid boots. Well fed.

'Ours. Ramage's. What's it to you? Either way I reckon you'd better fuck off.'

The girl is standing behind Kas now, her arms folded tight across her chest. 'I'm not yours, not anybody's,' she says, her voice defiant.

The Wilder with the sneer and the black gums takes a step

150

towards us but stops when we both aim at his heart.

'You've got no idea,' he says. 'Ramage'll hunt you down, especially when he hears about the ugly sister bein' alive.'

Kas steps up to him and jams the barrel of her rifle under his chin, forcing him to stand on his tiptoes.

He smiles and licks his lips. 'You as feisty as your sister, girlie? I heard she was all right.'

Kas moves quickly, bringing her knee up into his balls. His legs buckle under him and he collapses to the ground. Kas stands over him pointing the rifle at his head. I've seen this look on her face before, anger and hate—and something else I can't explain. Her jaw is set hard and she's breathing heavy.

'I remember you, Sweeney. I remember what you did in Longley,' she snarls. 'I'd kill you but you're not worth the bullet.'

Sweeney tries to roll away but Kas follows him.

I reach over to her and slowly pull the barrel away from Sweeney's head. He crawls backwards, swearing loudly.

The other two Wilders back away.

Jack has them covered. 'On your knees,' he shouts. They cower in front of him. 'Finn,' he says. 'Check their bags for some rope.'

'They have cable ties.' It's the girl. I notice her accent. She sort of clips the end off each word.

She's right. I find half a dozen short ties and one long one. While I cover the Wilders, Jack forces them to stand back to back. Sweeney can't hold himself upright yet but Jack yanks him to his feet. He uses the shorter ties to fasten their wrists, then he runs the long tie through all the shorter ones.

'We won't be able to keep up with you like this,' Sweeney says.

'You're right,' Jack says. 'That's why we're leaving you here.'

'You'll pay for this,' Sweeney spits.

'I doubt it,' Jack says, rummaging through their bags, looking for anything useful. 'But, just in case'—he gets to his feet and stands in front of them—'we might make it a bit harder for you.' He smiles and thuds his rifle into the side of their legs. They fall on top of each other. Then, one foot at a time, Jack takes off their boots, checks them for size against his own and pushes them into his pack.

'I know some people who'll appreciate these,' he says.

The girl has moved away towards the trees, ready to run. Kas lowers her rifle and approaches her. 'What's your name?' she asks.

The girl hesitates, still unsure of us. 'Daymu,' she says.

'She's a Siley,' Sweeney yells. 'A runaway. We've tracked her from Longley. She's ours.'

Kas looks back at him. I'm worried she'll kill him if he keeps this up. I place myself between them and point my rifle at Sweeney. 'Shut the fuck up,' I say, trying to sound vicious.

But Sweeney just laughs and makes a barking noise.

'You think you scare me, boy? Look at you, weak as piss. Ramage has a price on your head for what you done to him. He'll make an example of you.'

'Weak as piss?' Jack says, getting to his feet and standing over Sweeney. 'I'll tell you who's weak as piss. Grown men who take advantage of young kids. You ought to be ashamed.'

'The world's different now, or haven't you noticed?' Sweeney says. 'There are no rules. No one can tell us what to do.'

'Ramage tells you what to do,' Kas cuts in. 'And you're stupid enough to follow him. That's weak as piss. You're pathetic.'

'Least I'm not a freak.'

'That's it?' she says, smiling now. 'That's the best you've got?'

'All right,' Jack says. 'We gotta get going.'

'What about them?' I ask, pointing at the Wilders.

'Them?' Jack says, laughing, 'They've got a long day ahead of them, probably a long week. And even if they do survive, I'm sure Ramage will be impressed they lost their prisoner.'

The Wilders have only the one weapon, a useless old shotgun with no ammunition as far as we can see. Just the same, Jack smashes it against a tree, warping the barrels and breaking the stock into pieces. Then we leave them and make our way into the bush. Daymu is uncertain about this new situation, but Kas encourages her. Before we go too far we stop and watch as the three Wilders try to get to their feet. They scrabble at the ground, swearing and cursing at each other. They won't be going anywhere for a while.

'What are we going to do with her?' Jack asks, looking at Daymu.

The girl shifts her gaze from one of us to another. 'I won't hold you up,' she says.

'What were you doing out here?' Kas asks.

'I didn't know where to go.'

'Where did you come from? Originally.'

'Wentworth.'

'You're from Wentworth?' I say. She looks at me strangely.

'It's okay,' Kas says, 'he talks like that all the time. You get used to it.'

Daymu nods. 'I lived there for a while, until it got too dangerous. My owners both died.'

I remember what the No-landers said about what was happening in Wentworth. I wonder if it was dangerous for everybody or just for Sileys.

Kas takes Daymu's left hand and turns it over to see the familiar lump under her skin. It's then we notice a large welt on the inside of her forearm. She tries to pull away, but Kas holds her. There is a dark 'R' burnt into her skin.

'What's this?' Kas asks.

Daymu looks at the ground. Her voice is almost a whisper. 'It's what they're doing at the feedstore, now.'

'Branding!' Kas says through clenched teeth. 'The bastards.'

Jack walks off a little, surveying the country ahead.

'You were in Longley?' Kas asks Daymu.

'Only for a few days,' she says. 'Things were happening there. They were getting ready to send raiding parties out once the weather cleared. I took my chance one night and escaped. I'd heard the kids in Longley talking about some Sileys who're fighting back. I was trying to find them.'

Before Kas or I can say anything about the No-landers, Jack says, 'We don't have time to talk. You can come with us or not. It's up to you. But we're leaving now.'

Daymu doesn't hesitate. 'I'll come,' she says.

15

We make good time, even though the terrain is rough. The bracken has been replaced by sword grass that slices at our bare arms. Daymu keeps up easily, though her legs below her dress are crisscrossed with cuts from the grass. She's small, but there's strength in her body. She doesn't push at the undergrowth, she turns sideways and seems to slip through the gaps.

After an hour or so, we stop to rest. Kas offers Daymu water. She takes a long drink then spills some of it into her hands and splashes her face, rubbing at the cut above her eye. She sits back against a log and draws her knees up to her chest. From a pocket in her dress she pulls a small length of baling twine, bunches her hair in her hands and ties it back into a ponytail.

Kas sits next to her. 'Where are you from?' she asks.

Daymu doesn't hesitate. 'I am Karen,' she says.

'Where's that?'

'Not where, what. My people are from Myanmar.'

'You came through the camps?'

'Yes, with my brother.'

'Where's he?'

Daymu hesitates, looking past us into the bush. 'We were separated. Then I was caught. I don't know where he is.'

I break up the last of the bread. Daymu wolfs hers down.

Without having to speak about it Kas and I have made a decision—not to tell her about the No-landers, not yet.

Before long, we turn south into the foothills, leaving the plains behind. A road winds through the thickening forest, rising with the ridges and falling away into little valleys with ruined farm-houses and open paddocks that are slowly being reclaimed by the bush. We move at an easy pace, Jack and me out in front, keeping our eyes peeled, especially in the open country, and Kas and Daymu following behind. The storms must have been less severe here. There are a few smaller trees across the road but mostly the way is clear.

It's approaching midday; the sun is high behind my left shoulder, when we reach the top of a hill and get our first view of Swan's Marsh. A couple of hundred metres ahead of us the road meets a larger one, coming from Longley.

Jack waits until Kas and Daymu catch up. 'Swan's Marsh,' he says, pointing towards the cluster of buildings sitting low in the valley. 'That's it. I'm heading back. Be careful. The Monahans are a rough mob. And they're in with Ramage. If they don't kill you, they'll hand you over to him. And you heard what the Wilders said: Ramage'll do anything to catch you two.'

I'd hoped Jack would stick around a bit longer.

'Sorry,' he says, his voice softer. 'I've got to get back to the valley before Ramage gets there. It's going to be a tough fight—we can't afford to be a man down.'

He shakes my hand and wishes me luck. There's an awkward moment when he stands in front of Kas, not sure whether to shake her hand too, or even hug her. Kas just nods and gives him a half smile.

'Stay off the roads,' he says. 'Another couple of days and the place could be swarming with Wilders.' He hitches his pack onto his back. It bulges with the Wilders' boots.

'Right then,' he says. 'I'm off.'

The three of us watch Jack disappear over the crest of the hill. It's been a while since we've been on our own. I don't know whether I'm relieved or worried.

We drop off the side of the road and find a protected spot in a stand of wattles. We have a clear view down to the town about half a kilometre away. The whole place looks deserted. There's no smoke rising from chimneys, no noise of chopping wood or hammering nails.

'What do you remember about coming through here on the way to the coast?' I ask Kas.

'Not much more than what Rose would've told you.'

'She said there was a general store on the main street,' I say. 'That's where the Monahans were.'

Daymu has been listening, trying to understand what I'm saying and follow the conversation.

'We need to get closer,' I say. 'Maybe in those trees behind the houses on the right.' Beyond the buildings on the left of the main street there's nothing but open paddocks, but on the right the bush pushes down from a small ridge to within twenty or thirty metres of the houses and shops. From Rose's description, the largest one of these, a weatherboard place with a bull-nosed verandah and an open yard next to it, is the general store.

Kas says, 'Daymu, can you stay here with the gear for a few minutes?'

Daymu nods.

Kas and I take the rifles and make our way down through the trees to the top of the paddock above the road. I'm not sure why she's brought us here. 'Do you remember the directions the No-landers gave us about getting to their place?' she asks.

'Yeah. But why do we need to go there? If we find Hope, we can take her straight to the valley.'

'Not us. Daymu. We could tell her where to find the No-landers.'

It seems like a good idea. We don't have enough food for three and we don't need another person to look out for.

'Okay,' I say. 'But if she tells them about us, they'll know we lied to them back at Pinchgut.'

'Yeah, I thought of that, too, but so what? We'll be on our way back to the valley before she even finds them.'

We climb back up to Daymu. I'm pretty sure she knows we're still suspicious of her.

'There's something we haven't told you,' Kas says. She recounts our meeting with the No-landers, without mentioning anything about them looking for Rose.

Daymu listens quietly, probably trying to figure out whether we're telling the truth or just trying to get rid of her. 'So, how can I find their farm?' she says.

We walk to the side of the paddock, looking to the north-west. I've been trying to get my bearings while Kas's been talking. 'I reckon you'll need to follow the road towards Longley for an hour or so. That'll be super dangerous, so be careful. There should be a creek flowing down off the ridges up there,' I say, pointing to the hills that rise to the blue-grey range that's catching the afternoon sun. 'Follow the creek upstream. You'll see a fire tower at the high point above the valley. Head towards it and you should find the No-landers, though they'll most likely find you first.'

Daymu is wide eyed. I'm not sure how much she understands of what I'm saying.

Kas opens her pack and pulls out the dried meat. She breaks some off and gives it to Daymu. 'It's not much, but…'

Daymu looks as though she's going to cry. 'Thank you,' she says.

'Hey,' says Kas. 'We Sileys have to stick together.' She rummages in the pack again and pulls out some clothes, a pair of shorts and a long-sleeved shirt. 'These'll be a bit big but they'll be warmer than that dress.'

Daymu takes them, feeling the material and holding them against her chest like they are the most precious things she's ever held. She hides behind a tree to change.

When she steps back out it's hard not to laugh. She's taken the baling twine out of her hair to loop around her waist and hold the shorts up and the shirt is a couple of sizes too big. She hitches the shorts and shrugs.

She bundles her dress up and wraps the meat in it, while we hide the packs in the branches of a fallen tree.

We walk parallel to the road until we come to the T-intersection. Moving is easier without the packs, but the rifles are awkward. We cross the road as quickly as we can and hide in the trees along its south side.

Daymu takes a few steps, then turns and says, 'Good luck. I won't forget you.'

Kas lifts her left hand, turning it to show her implant. Daymu does the same, then moves off warily, scanning up and down the road. When she's satisfied it's clear, she steps out onto the bitumen and starts running.

It takes Kas and me about ten minutes to reach the first building, a burnt-out brick house. From here we have some cover until we're within sight of the general store. Then we head uphill into the trees and find a spot that gives a good view of the yard and the back door.

We sit, watch and wait. Kas fidgets, her leg jerking up and down. I put my hand on her knee. 'Sorry,' she says. 'I've never been good at sitting still. Hope could be down there.'

I'm battling to keep my own nerves under control. After the peaceful days in the valley this is serious again.

After about an hour, Kas has had enough. 'I think we should go down,' she says. 'We would've seen something by now if they were here.'

The old familiar adrenaline starts to pump through my body. Carrying the rifles in front of us, we run and slide down to a paling fence at the back of the yard. Somewhere off to our right a dog barks, the first sign of life in the town.

Kas signals for us to make a run to the back of the store. I pull a couple of the palings aside to open a gap. Kas slips through but my jumper gets caught when I try to follow. She comes back to unhook me, looking over her shoulder at the house. Just as I get loose, we hear the back door open. The flyscreen bangs against the side of the house.

It's Bridget Monahan.

She freezes when she sees us, dropping the washing basket she's holding and looking back over her shoulder. Kas and I stop dead in our tracks and there's a moment when all the sound around us seems to die.

Bridget steps out and closes the door carefully behind her, holding a finger to her lips. She shoos us around the corner of the house. We're caught between turning and running or following her signal. Kas is the first to move—towards the house. I follow and we crouch under a big bush growing against the back wall. Bridget picks up her basket and walks past us to the washing line.

Without turning to look at us, she whispers, 'Don't move.'

We can hear voices inside the house, now.

She begins to hang out the washing.

The back door opens and a man's voice calls, 'You know where the shed key is, Mum?'

'Where it always is, dumb-arse. On the hook by the fire.' Her voice is casual.

When she's finished the washing, she wanders back towards us. Leaning against the wall, her voice low and hurried now, she says, 'There's a church this side of the street, couple of hundred metres. Wait for me there. I'll come after dark.'

She walks back around the corner and we hear the door open and close. I've been holding my breath, pushing my body back against the wall.

'Come on, let's go,' Kas says.

We follow the wall along the side of the house, climb a low brick fence and run back up towards the trees. My heart's in my mouth and my breath is coming in gulps. It's hard to run with the rifle. I almost wish I hadn't brought it.

When we reach the trees we drop to the ground. '*Shit,*' Kas says, 'that was close.'

'Can we trust her?'

'Maybe.'

'She could've given us away, but she didn't.'

The conversation goes back and forth like this for a while. In the end, we decide we need to know what's happened to Hope, so we have to meet her in the church.

'There's one thing I don't like,' Kas says.

'What?'

'Did you see the washing on the line?'

'Yeah. So what?'

'There were no baby clothes.'

16

Once the sun drops behind the hills to the west, the valley starts to cool. It's an hour off sunset, but we make our way along the back of the buildings until we can see the church. There's not much left of it. The stained-glass windows along one side have been pushed out and they lie in coloured pieces on the ground. Two doors hang by their hinges, looking as though they've been attacked with axes.

When darkness finally comes, we approach the church from the back, listening for any sound that might spell danger. Inside, it's almost empty. All the pews are gone, probably for firewood; even some of the floorboards have been pulled up. The place is littered with leaves and over in one corner there's a pile of moth-eaten blankets and a dirty pillow.

There's a small space behind where the altar must have been. We squeeze ourselves in there, sit with our backs to the wall and wait.

It's not long before we hear footsteps on the wooden floor. I peer around the corner to see Bridget Monahan, her red hair frizzing around her head like she's walked through a storm. She's carrying a rifle.

'You there?' she whispers.

We step out slowly. She raises her gun then lowers it when she sees ours pointed to the floor.

'Come closer,' she says. 'I can't make you out.'

We walk towards her, careful to avoid the gaps in the floor.

'So,' she says, 'you two must be either brave or stupid, coming here.'

'We don't want trouble,' Kas says, her voice firm.

'If you didn't want trouble, luv, you should've stayed where you were. There's a price on both your young heads.'

'The baby,' Kas says. 'We've come for the baby.'

'Yeah, well,' Bridget sighs, 'I didn't think you'd come for afternoon tea.'

'Where is she?' Kas insists.

'Slow down, luv.' She eases her weight onto one hip and tilts her head a little. 'I'm sorry for what happened. If I'd got there earlier I might've been able to save your sister.'

Kas meets her gaze. 'We did the best we could,' she says.

The woman makes a *tsk-tsk* sound. 'And you,' she says,

pointing her chin at me, 'you've made yourself an enemy. Benny, Mister Ramage, he wants you most of all. You tried to kill him. *Big* mistake.'

I'm getting a squirming feeling in my gut. The hairs on my arms are standing up. She's stalling us.

'Where's the baby?' I say. 'Where's Hope?'

'Hope. That's a nice name. Mister Ramage called her Shauna, after his wife.'

'Where is she?' Kas's voice is urgent now. Something's not right about this meeting, the way Bridget looks so comfortable standing here talking to us in secret.

'She's not here. We went back to Longley for a while. I looked after her, little mite that she is. She cried a lot, though, and Benny didn't like that. There was a Siley of his, young girl, just lost her baby so Benny gave Shauna to her and sent them to live in another part of town. The Ramsay place. Guards them night and day.'

'How do we know you're telling the truth?' Kas says.

'Well, that's it, luv, you don't. But right at the moment, I don't think that matters much.'

She turns her head as though she's listening for something then slowly brings her rifle up until it's pointing at us.

We lift ours quickly, but two heavy figures appear in the doorway and another leans through the open window.

They've all got guns.

'Sorry, kids,' Bridget says, 'but Mister Ramage will pay well for you two and I have to look after my own first. They're family, after all.' Her voice hasn't lost its singsong kindliness but the smile has left her face and her mouth turns down at the edges. 'It's a pity, I miss having young people around.'

A much harsher voice, deep and menacing, a man's voice, says, 'Put your guns down slowly and step back. I'm not as nice as my mum. I'll shoot if ya make me.'

Kas is breathing heavily and I'm sure my heart is beating loud enough for everyone to hear.

We place our rifles on the floor and step away from them.

Another man comes in from our left and picks up the guns. He stands in front of us, cradling them in his arms. He's huge, as big as Fenton and as wide as Kas and me put together.

The other one in the doorway lights a lamp and brings it over to us. Our hands are pulled behind our backs and tied tight until the rope burns.

There's no conversation. We're hustled out into the street and back to the general store. Inside, we're pushed into a windowless room and the door is locked behind us. Then we hear them in the next room.

Bridget is calling the shots, the others waiting on her instructions.

'Joey, take Griff. Ride quick as you can to Longley and tell Ramage what's happened.'

'Why don't we just take them ourselves?' a deeper voice asks.

'We're not giving them up for nothing. I want enough supplies for a year, at least. He can send his men out here to negotiate.'

'That's a dangerous game, Mum. You know what he's like.'

Her voice is firm. 'We're on his side. We're valuable, guarding the road. We need to be looked after.'

'She's right.' It's the deep voice again. 'He needs us out here, especially with them Sileys on the loose and fighting back.'

Kas has found me in the dark, her shoulder touching mine. She hasn't said anything since the ambush in the church. 'Sileys,' she whispers. 'Must be the No-landers.'

There's the sound of pots and pans in the kitchen, heavy footsteps moving around the house and, every now and again, Bridget giving orders. Eventually, the smell of cooking meat finds its way into our room. We've hardly eaten all day and my stomach is rumbling.

Our eyes start to adapt to the dark and I make out Kas worrying away at the ropes behind her back.

'*Shit*,' she says. '*Shit, shit, shit*,' her voice is quiet but frantic.

I know we've stuffed up, but maybe I'm getting more used to being in tough situations. It doesn't mean I'm not scared, but I know there's nothing to be gained from panicking.

'Hey, ease up,' I say. 'We gotta think our way through this.'

'We walked into a trap, Finn. It was stupid. They're going to hand us over to Ramage.'

'I know. It doesn't mean we can't be smart now, though.'

'How?'

'We know they're sending someone to get the Wilders. They're going to try to bargain with Ramage. That gives us a little bit of time. We have to keep alert for any chance we get.'

Just as I say this, a key turns in the lock and the room is flooded with light. We see a mattress in the far corner and a large bowl that looks like a piss pot. Two men lift us to our feet and walk us out into the kitchen. One unties the ropes around our wrists and the other picks up a rifle from the corner by the stove and rests it in his arms. Bridget is working at the stove. She doesn't bother turning around.

'When did you last eat?' she asks.

'Had a little bit this morning,' I say.

The two men look like father and son. The older one has a grizzled beard streaked with grey. He could be fifty or seventy, it's hard to tell. The younger one's probably in his thirties, the same round face as his father, his cheeks red with veins close to the surface. I'm guessing they're drinkers, probably some rotgut they're making themselves.

'Tom and Joey,' Bridget says without us asking.

She places a big pot in the middle of the table and starts to ladle watery soup into bowls.

'Wallaby,' she says. 'It's not much but it'll fill your gut. Don't want Ramage thinking we haven't looked after you.'

The big guy from the church comes in, stooping to avoid hitting his head on the doorframe. He sits at one end of the table. Bridget is at the other end and Joey and Tom sit opposite us. Joey stands the rifle against his chair, with the barrel sticking up far enough to remind us it's there.

'So,' Joey says, the fat from the soup greasing his moustache, 'which one of you's the horse thief?'

Kas looks up from her bowl.

'I thought so,' he says. 'He's a bastard to ride, isn't he. Needs a good flogging to keep him in line.'

'Yogi?' Kas says, her eyes wide.

'What sorta name's that for a horse? His name's Griff.'

'But how?'

'One of Ramage's raiding parties found him on the coast before the winter,' Joey says. 'Not much left of him by the time they got him up here, all skin and bone. Took a lot of convincing to stop them killing and eating him.'

I can't help myself. 'Was there an old man with them when they came back? Grey hair, beard, walks kinda funny?'

'Not that I saw,' Joey says.

'That's enough,' Tom cuts in. 'They don't need to know all that. They're prisoners, remember.'

'Means nothing to them, now,' Joey says. 'The boy'll be dead within the week and Ramage'll have plans for the girl. Pity about that mark on her face. She'd be a looker without it.'

The soup is salty and thin but there's a bit of meat on the bones and I eat it all. It does nothing to stop the sick feeling in my stomach.

Bridget finishes hers and pushes her bowl away. 'What were you thinking? You must've known Ramage was after you. And even if you found the baby, what then? She's too young for you to look after.'

I'm struggling to match the woman in front of me with the one that helped Rose escape. Is the big guy at the end of the table who hasn't said a word the one she hit over the head with a shovel? I want to ask but as soon as we've finished our bowls we're bundled back into the room. At least they haven't tied our hands this time. We find each other in the dark and feel our way to the mattress in the corner. It stinks of something, rat or maybe possum, but it's more comfortable than the floor.

We sit on it, with our backs up against the wall.

'Yogi's here,' Kas says. 'He's alive.'

'Yeah, not sure that's going to help us, though.'

'It was dumb to think we could trust Bridget.'

'Easy to say, but we had to find out about Hope.'

We've got no energy left to talk. We lie down on the mattress. It's not much, but at least we have each other.

Then her voice comes soft and low in the dark. 'Finn?'

'Yeah.'

'Ray's dead.'

'Maybe, but I'm not going to give up until I know for sure.'

The next afternoon, the Wilders arrive. I listen carefully for Ramage's trail bike but I don't hear it. Maybe he hasn't come. There are new voices in the kitchen and the sound of an argument. Bridget is negotiating.

'Fair's fair,' she says. 'You never would've caught them if it wasn't for us.'

There's the sound of chairs scraping on the floor and a louder, harsher voice. Kas's hand grabs my arm.

It's Tusker.

'You think Ramage gives a stuff about fair?' he demands. 'We're taking them to Longley, and that's it.'

Tom enters the argument. 'We did the right thing. We sent word to Ramage. Joey rode hard to get the message to you.'

Tusker isn't impressed. 'You Monahans are up yourselves. This is Ramage country. Think yourselves lucky we let you stay here at all.'

'We're not asking for much,' Bridget says, 'just supplies to see us through. Some food, a bit of ammo.'

'You'll get whatever Ramage thinks they're worth. We're leaving here with them, as soon as we get a decent feed.'

'We don't have any food to spare,' Tom says, his voice nervous but angry, like he's not sure how far he can press his case.

'Well, you'd better find some. We're not going to travel on empty stomachs. In the meantime, you can show us where they are.'

We move back and stand in the middle of the room. As the key turns in the lock, I reach for Kas's hand and we hold on tight.

Tusker's big frame is silhouetted in the doorway. He steps in and stands in front of us, arms folded. 'I knew you'd come. Couldn't help yourselves, could you?'

We do our best to hold our ground but he leans down, his face close enough for Kas to reel back with the stench of him. 'You bitch,' he spits, touching his hand to his ear, 'I'm gonna make you pay.'

Two more Wilders come into the room. They pull us apart. One grabs me by the throat and pins me to the wall, and the other holds Kas's arms from behind. Tusker's great paw runs down the side of her face then he clamps her by the jaw and squeezes. Kas struggles.

'You see this?' he says, turning to show his disfigured ear. 'You should've had more respect.'

Kas plants her feet and tries to work her way free but the Wilder pulls her arms tighter behind her back.

'Don't hurt her, Jimmy,' Tusker says. 'We don't want damaged goods, now do we? I want her in tip-top shape when we get back to Longley.'

The Wilder laughs.

'You see,' Tusker continues, pulling Kas's face even closer, 'me and Benny Ramage, we've come to a little agreement. If I bring him your boyfriend here, I get you.'

He grins and the scar creases up the side of his face. Then his hand traces Kas's body, down to her hip.

Bridget appears in the door behind him. 'There's some grub ready.' She doesn't look at me or Kas.

I'm praying Kas isn't going to say anything to provoke him. She doesn't—but she spits in his face. He raises his hand to hit her but holds himself back. He just smiles and wipes his face with his sleeve.

The Wilder throws her onto the mattress, and he and Tusker walk out into the kitchen. The one pinning me to the wall punches me hard in the stomach and I collapse. He locks the door behind him, leaving me gasping for breath and Kas huddled on the mattress.

When I can move again, I crawl over to Kas. She is trembling. I can't tell if it's from anger or fear, or both.

17

Within an hour, our wrists are bound behind us and we're marched out through the kitchen to the yard. We both squint against the light. There are six Wilders, including Tusker, standing in a half-circle. Tom, the big guy, and Bridget are off to the side. Joey is nowhere to be seen.

'Let's get moving,' Tusker says. 'Where's that halfwit son of yours?'

As he speaks, Joey walks into the yard, leading a horse.

It's Yogi.

Kas can't hold herself back. She breaks free of the Wilder restraining her and runs towards Yogi.

Tusker shakes his head.

Attached to the ties around her wrists is a length of rope. The Wilder braces and pulls on it. Kas's body lifts off the ground and she falls heavily on her back, her arms trapped underneath her.

The Wilders laugh.

Kas struggles to her feet. Yogi drops his head and nudges her. 'Hello, boy,' she says. 'Hello, Yogi Bear.'

'See that, boys?' Tusker snorts. 'Doesn't it melt your heart?'

The Wilder pulls Kas back in by the rope and Joey drags Yogi away.

'Thanks, son,' Tusker says, taking the reins from Joey. He lifts himself into the saddle and pulls hard on the reins. 'I'll teach him who's boss along the way.'

Yogi skitters sideways, but Tusker stays with him. 'Save your energy, you bag of shit. We got a long way to go today,' he says.

Kas can't look as Tusker slides out of the saddle and Joey hands him a riding crop. He raises it high and hits Yogi across his flank and neck. The horse rears away but Tusker pulls him back and holds him on a tight rein.

'You see that, girl,' he yells at Kas, 'that's how you train a horse.'

Finally, he drags himself back up into the saddle and slides the crop into his boot. 'Now,' he says, 'let's get this show on the road.' He wheels Yogi around and out onto the main street.

The Wilders move off after him, with Kas and me wedged in the middle of them.

As we shuffle past Bridget, she can't meet our eyes. She turns and walks back into the house.

We move at a quick pace. The Wilders make no attempt to hide themselves. This is their country and they're comfortable in it. Tusker slouches in the saddle, sometimes whistling but more often barking at his men to get a move on.

It's not easy to walk fast with your hands tied behind your back, and the Wilders kick us every so often to speed up. We pass the road junction where we left Daymu and we both avoid looking up to the stand of wattles that hides our packs.

The afternoon drags. We've barely eaten in two days and our bodies are weak. But Tusker takes few rests, usually only when his men complain.

Towards nightfall, we take a longer break at a bridge where a creek flows down from the main range. Kas and I have to kneel down and put our faces into the water to drink. When we stand up we both peer through the trees looking for any sign of the fire tower that marks the No-landers farm. But the hazy dusk limits how far we can see.

I notice now that each time we stop Tusker posts sentries at the edges of the group. They are much more wary out here than they were back closer to Swan's Marsh.

As I'm looking around, I hear a birdcall I've never heard before—two high-pitched whistles that might be a hawk of some kind. It comes from the hills behind us. Then an answering call follows from the other side of the valley, this time three whistles. Kas has heard it, too. None of the Wilders seems to notice.

Tusker dismounts and allows Yogi to drink. He ties him to the railing on the bridge then comes over and squats next to us. His eyes scan upriver. 'You know anything about these Sileys out here?' he asks, his voice low, almost friendly.

'What Sileys?' Kas says.

'Runaways. We'll track them down soon enough, now the weather's turned. The world's a dangerous place these days. I don't know why anyone wouldn't want Ramage's protection.'

'Protection!' Kas spits.

Tusker snorts. 'Sileys don't belong here in the first place. They should be grateful for anything we give them.'

'Locked up, abused, starved, killed? Yeah, why wouldn't we be grateful?'

'Anything's better than the shitholes you come from.' The edge has returned to Tusker's voice.

Kas wants to keep him talking. It gives us more time to rest. 'Why are you so surprised Sileys are fighting back? You'd do the same in their position.'

Tusker doesn't answer, but he pauses for a few seconds before saying, 'We'll hunt them down. If they fight us, we'll kill them.'

'That's still better than being a slave,' Kas says.

We walk on into the night, both of us stumbling from exhaustion. I'm sure I hear the bird call again a couple of times. The same pattern—two calls answered by three.

Eventually we see the buildings of Longley start to take shape in the dark. As we get closer to the centre of town, a man holding a lantern steps out of a house and watches us pass.

He hisses and whistles at Kas.

Tusker laughs, 'Ease up boys. She's mine.'

We turn into the wide main street, and Tusker stops outside some high gates that are topped with barbed wire. Attached to the fence is rusty sign: 'Ramage's Stock and Feed'.

'Welcome home,' Tusker says, leaning down close to Kas. 'Don't worry, though, you won't be here long. You'll be moving into my place soon enough.'

We are pushed inside the yard. One of the Wilders cuts the ties around our wrists and the gates are locked behind us. My hands are numb and I have to rub them on my legs to get some feeling back into them. There's a large shed in the corner of the yard. Half a dozen figures stand by the open door. As we draw closer one rushes towards us.

'*Kas*,' she cries and throws her arms around her.

'Danka!'

They walk arm in arm through the big sliding door. Inside there's the smell of hay and fertiliser and shit, all mixed together. A lamp is lit and we're led to a long wooden table underneath a loft. There must be fifteen or twenty people here, crowding in.

Danka speaks in a thick, unfamiliar accent. 'This is Kas. And—'

'Finn,' Kas says.

Questions are thrown at us from all directions. 'Where have you come from? How were you caught? What's happening outside Longley? Where's Rose?'

Kas catches this last question and looks up at the girl who asked it. 'Rose is dead,' she says, and everyone falls quiet.

The girl puts her hand to her mouth.

'She died last autumn,' Kas says.

'And her baby?' Danka asks.

'Alive, but she's been brought back here somewhere. A girl. Hope.'

'It must be the baby Sylvia is looking after,' Danka says.

Kas grabs her by the arm. 'Where's Sylvia?' she asks.

'We haven't seen her since before the winter.'

'Does anyone know the Ramsay place?' I say. It's the farm Bridget Monahan mentioned. Everyone turns to look at me.

'I know the Ramsay farm.' It's a boy's voice, coming from the back of the group. They open up and let him through. He's a thickset kid, maybe twelve or thirteen, with tight dark curls and brown skin. 'It's the last place along the main road before the railway. I worked there last year.'

Kas shoots a glance at me. I nod. At least we know where Hope is. But first we have to get out of here.

'What's been happening here?' Kas asks. 'Where's Ramage? Have there been any escapes?'

'Vashti escaped, before the winter,' Danka begins, talking over the others. 'Food's been scarce but they still forced us out to work, even in the storms. Nothing much has grown. We haven't had meat in three months.'

'Longer,' a voice calls from the back.

'But the last couple of weeks, they've been getting raiding parties together, heading out in groups of four or five. And there's been another escape.'

'I think we met her.' Kas says. 'Daymu?'

All the voices rise again. 'Where? Was she okay? Has she found her brother?'

Kas tells them about the Wilders capturing Daymu and how we helped her. A little cheer ripples through the group. It turns to laughter when she tells them how Jack tied the Wilders up and took their boots.

She doesn't say anything about the No-landers. We're careful, now, about who we trust.

'What about Ramage?' I ask.

'He was here until yesterday. There was a big carry on when one of his men came back from somewhere to the east. He was all cut up and looked like he'd been in a fight.'

'Douglas!' I say, and they all turn to look at me. I can't tell if it's because of what I've said or the sound of my voice.

'How do you know his name?' Danka says.

'Doesn't matter. What happened then?'

'They took every man they could spare,' Danka says, 'maybe a dozen of them. Headed off in the middle of the night. Ramage waited until the morning, then followed on his trail bike.'

'How many are left here?' Kas asks.

'Not sure, but we've only seen four. Plus the ones that came with you,' Danka says.

'Douglas?'

'Still here.'

Kas and I look at each other, both thinking the same thing. Douglas will want revenge after the way he was treated in the valley.

We're so tired we can hardly keep our eyes open. Danka

tells the others to give us some space.

'Have you eaten?' she asks us.

'Not a scrap,' I say.

'We don't have much but...'

She gets to her feet and walks off into the dark, returning after a few minutes with a couple of limp looking carrots.

'Sorry,' she says, 'but it's all we've got. You won't believe what we've eaten this winter. Horse feed. Chook pellets. Anything we can smuggle back from the farms.'

We're led up into the loft where hay bales are arranged to form rough rooms. There are hessian sacks to throw over the top of us, and thick hay to lie on. We hardly notice, collapsing onto the makeshift beds.

'Where do I remember Danka's name from,' I whisper to Kas.

'She's the one I told you had the baby Rose and me helped to deliver last year.'

Before I drift off I hear Kas say, 'Danka?'

'What?'

'Where's your baby?'

The silence is our answer.

We're woken in the morning by conversation at the table below us. It sounds as though everyone is up. We've had our best sleep since leaving the valley.

'I'm scared of Tusker,' Kas says, her voice low.

I put an arm around her but I can't find any words to comfort her. At least Ramage isn't here, but he could return any day. I hope the farmers can stall him in the valley.

'There must be a way out,' I say. 'Daymu escaped.'

We climb down from the loft and join the others at the table. They're a hotchpotch of ages, shapes, sizes and colours. I count fourteen altogether. And, in the daylight, I see they all have an 'R' branded on their forearms.

'Are you still being sent out to work the farms?' Kas asks.

A boy they call Sammy answers. 'Not much in the last week with all the commotion. We've been locked in here. Pretty much forgotten about. But that might change now, with Tusker back. He's a mean piece of shit.'

The others murmur their agreement. Some of the girls link arms and hold each other.

'How did Daymu escape?' I ask.

A tall blond boy, about my age, answers. 'There was a fight between two Wilders,' he says. 'It happens all the time. When they get tired of beating us up, they turn on each other. We didn't even notice Daymu was gone until the next morning when we saw a couple of the Wilders mending a tiny gap in the fence. She was small enough to slip through.'

This gets me thinking about how well they guard the fences. We'll need to watch how often they patrol, especially at night.

Looking more closely at the kids, none of them looks well. Some have sores on their skin, most are thinner than they should be. All of them have long, matted hair and some scratch constantly at their scalps.

Danka sees me looking. 'Lice,' she says. 'Big enough to eat!'

'Show me outside,' I say to Danka, motioning Kas to follow. The yard is a big rectangle, taking up half the block. There

182

are no trees, no shade of any sort, and the ground is a mix of concreted areas and gravel. One side is dominated by a two-storey brick building, the feedstore office, with a line of windows overlooking the yard. We clearly see Tusker and Douglas looking down at us. Douglas is pointing.

We turn our backs to them.

'What's up?' Danka asks, realising I wasn't keen to talk in front of the others.

'Kas and I are pretty sure we were followed last night.'

'Followed? Who by?'

I glance at Kas and she nods. So I tell Danka about the meeting with the No-landers and how Daymu set out to look for them.

'We've heard the Wilders talk about them,' Danka says. 'Ramage is worried. They've been hitting some of his smaller farms, taking food, stock, weapons. Ramage thinks he knows the area they are in but up until now he hasn't been able to find them.'

'They know how to stay out of sight,' Kas says.

'We're pretty sure Ramage was getting a big search party together, but then Douglas arrived and plans changed,' Danka says.

Again, Kas and I exchange glances.

'What aren't you telling me?' Danka asks.

Kas takes over the story, telling her about the valley.

'So Tusker came from there?' Danka says. 'And he's a traitor. Doesn't surprise me. He's not so bad when Ramage is about, spends most of his time crawling up his arse, but when Ramage is away, he takes advantage. That's when he's at his worst.'

'Like now, you mean?' and we all turn and look up at the windows. There's no sign of Tusker or Douglas.

18

Some time around midday, there's the sound of the chain on the gate being moved and the squeal of rusty hinges. Everyone in the shed moves quickly out into the yard. Two Wilders with rifles guard another carrying a big cast-iron pot. He puts it down just inside the gate and they retreat, drawing the chain through and padlocking the gate. Then they stand back and watch.

'Here, piggy piggy,' one of the Wilders calls. 'Come and get your swill.'

Danka stands in front and whispers to the others, 'Just cos they treat us like pigs, doesn't mean we have to act like pigs.

Sammy, you and JT go and get it. Don't spill any.' JT is the tall boy who spoke at the table this morning. He and Sammy move quickly towards the gate. While they do, the Wilders have a competition to see who can spit over the top of the wire into the pot. When the boys get there, they shield the pot with their bodies, copping the spit in their hair and on their clothes. They don't respond, just walk back to the shed.

Inside, the pot is placed on the table. Everyone crowds around with a variety of spoons and bowls. Danka uses a tin cup to ladle out the soupy mixture. It looks like dirty water but towards the bottom there are some slimy vegetables.

'Turnips,' Danka says.

Late in the afternoon, the gate is opened again and three Wilders file through, two holding rifles and one with a long stick that has a knife taped to the end. Douglas follows them. He's wearing thick gloves and carrying a heavy metal bucket. There's smoke coming out the top. Next, Tusker steps through the gate holding a stiff length of wire.

'Oh, shit, no,' JT says, looking at me and Kas.

We are all called out into the yard. The sky is thickening with grey cloud and a cold wind whistles through the gaps in the buildings.

Tusker stands in front of us with his legs spread, his thumbs hitched into his belt. His eye twitches where the scar runs through it.

'Time for a bit of branding,' he says. 'So we know who belongs to who.'

He's looking at me.

'Step out here, dog boy. Be quick now. Woof, woof.'

All the Wilders laugh. 'My friend Dougie, here,' he says, 'tells me that you and my new girlfriend...' He pauses and glares at Kas. 'You killed his mates. And not just his mates, Rat! Ramage's son. Now, as you'd expect'—he's enjoying himself, making the moment last—'Benny Ramage will deal with you when he gets back from cleaning up the mess you left in the valley. But until then, I'm in charge of the branding.'

Douglas's bucket is half filled with glowing coals. Tusker pushes the end of the wire into the bucket and stands back with his arms folded. 'I think we'll let Dougie do the honours on you, boy.'

I can't stop my body shaking. My eyes are fixed on the bucket.

'Why c-can't I d-do the g-girl,' he says.

'Cos you'll do what I say, you idiot.'

Somewhere out past the gate, I hear the bird call, same as yesterday, high and shrill. Then the response.

Kas steps forward and links her arm in mine. 'It wasn't Finn. I killed Rat,' she says, defiant. 'And Wilson. I shot him. And I'd do it again.'

'Get out of the way, girl,' Tusker says. 'I don't want you scarred anymore than you are already.' He pushes Kas to the side and kicks me in the back of the legs to bring me to my knees. Then he wrenches my left arm, turns it over and stands on my hand, pinning it to the gravel.

From down here I can see through the legs of the Wilders.

There's movement behind them, over near the gate they've left open. A dozen No-landers slide through the gate, all with guns.

I struggle and kick at the ground but Tusker keeps my arm pinned.

Douglas is in a hurry. He pulls the wire from the bucket. The end is glowing red. He smiles as he presses it hard into my skin. The pain rips through my whole body. I scream. Tusker lifts his foot and I roll away, hugging my arm to my chest.

Douglas squats beside me, waving the hot wire in front of my face. 'W-weak as—'

He never gets to finish his sentence. A shot cracks the air and he slumps to the gravel.

All the kids scatter and the Wilders spin around towards the gate.

Tusker is unarmed but he tries to prise a weapon out of the hands of one of the others. As they wrestle another shot rings out, this time above their heads. The No-landers walk towards the Wilders, guns raised.

Through my tears, I recognise Tahir and Gabriel at the front. And, to the left of them, Daymu.

'On the ground!' Tahir shouts.

Tusker and the other three Wilders freeze, realising they're outnumbered. More No-landers push through the gate and all the feedstore kids stand up to crowd in.

The Wilders sink to their knees. Danka takes the rifle from Tusker's grasp.

The kids eye the No-landers warily. JT is the first to recognise Daymu. She runs to him and they embrace. Danka appears beside me with a bottle of water. She takes my hand and pours it over the wound. I can't look at it.

'So, my friends, we meet again,' Tahir says. His broad, white smile disappears when he sees my arm. More of the feedstore kids are bringing water but nothing eases the scorching pain of the burn.

'We tracked you yesterday,' Gabriel says, kneeling beside me. 'We had to wait for them to drop their guard. I'm sorry we didn't get here earlier.'

'We heard your calls,' Kas says.

'Yes. We saw you looking.'

Kas and Danka do some quick introductions. The Wilders have been made to lie on the ground, their hands on the backs of their heads. 'There are more of them in town,' Danka says. 'No time to stand around talking. And we've got to look after Finn's arm.'

The Wilders are cable-tied and taken behind the shed, out of sight. There's every chance others have heard the shots and will come to investigate.

The kids and the No-landers assemble in the shed. The space is tight—there must be more than thirty of us. Danka, Tahir and JT climb the ladder to the loft so they can see everyone.

Kas has brought me a bucket of water. I sit it on the table and put my arm in until the burn is covered. For the first time, I take a close look at it. The skin is raw around the black 'R' and the swelling radiates out towards my wrist and elbow. I push my hand hard against the bottom of the bucket to stop it shaking. Kas is beside me, rubbing my back. There are tears in her eyes.

It's started to rain. The heavy drops beat on the corrugated iron roof and Danka has to raise her voice to be heard. 'We're free but we'll have to move fast to get clear of town before Ramage finds out.'

She looks to Tahir and nods. He stands tall, the tattoos on his neck rising out of his shirt. 'You are welcome to join us,' he says. 'We are striking back at Ramage. We want to live our own lives, free of fear. But we've only won a small battle here. The war is yet to come.'

The other No-landers cheer.

'We are safer together,' he continues. 'We can organise, strike Ramage when he least expects it. We hunt for food, we have cattle and we grow crops. You will need to work and, when the time comes, to fight. We are leaving now. Gather what you have and come to the yard.'

Conversations break out all over the shed. Kids are running to get whatever they have—mostly clothes and chaff bags to keep them covered at night. I watch all this activity through blurred eyes. The water isn't doing much to ease the throbbing pain in my arm.

Tahir climbs down the ladder and confronts Kas and me. 'You lied to us about your sister,' he says, his voice hard.

'I know,' Kas says, meeting his gaze squarely. 'At the time, that was necessary.'

Tahir sizes her up. 'Will you come with us?' he asks.

'No. We're heading back to the valley. Our friends there

will need us.'

I'm sure Tahir is about to challenge her, but Gabriel calls to him from the door. 'Come on. We don't have time to argue.'

Tahir backs away, his finger pointing at Kas. 'Why don't I trust you?' he says.

'Probably the same reason I don't trust you,' she fires back.

Daymu has been watching this exchange. She still wears the shorts and jumper Kas gave her back at Swan's Marsh.

'I told you I wouldn't forget you,' she says, smiling.

JT stands beside her, his arm around her shoulder.

'We're coming with you,' JT says. 'You'll have a better chance with four than with two.' He has one of the Wilders' rifles.

Kas nods. She touches my shoulder and says, 'Let's look at your arm.' She lifts it gently out of the water. The movement shoots pain right up to my shoulder.

'It'll hurt like shit for a week, but then it gets easier,' JT says. He produces a jar of grey-white cream that smells like sheep's wool. 'They gave us this when they started the branding. Put it on everyday. It'll help.'

I smear the cold cream on the wound then bind it with a strip of cloth JT gives me. Somehow it doesn't feel quite as bad if I can't see it.

'We've got to get going,' JT says.

'There's something I have to do first,' Kas says. We follow her out of the shed and round the back. Tusker is propped up against the wall, his hands pinned behind his back. The other Wilders sit further along, their heads bowed.

Kas squats in front of Tusker. She pulls a knife from her belt and lifts his chin with the point. Her voice is calm, measured. 'There's something I want you to remember,' she says. 'You will never, *ever* own me.' Kas turns the knife so the blade begins to cut under his chin. She flicks it forward, opening a gash an inch long. Blood drops onto his shirt.

'That's from Yogi,' she says, standing up again.

'You should finish me now,' Tusker yells. 'Take your chance. Cos when I catch you—and, believe me, I *will* catch you—I'll kill you. And I will enjoy every minute of it.'

But Kas just smiles. 'Catch me?' she snorts. 'You'll never catch me. I'll smell you coming.'

She turns and walks towards me, then stops and backtracks. 'And one more thing,' she says, looking down on him. 'You're the ugliest bastard I've ever seen.'

Back in the yard, Gabriel leads the kids and the No-landers out through the gates and they form a ragged group hurrying off down the main street. Danka is the last to leave. She hugs Kas and Daymu.

'Stay safe,' she says. 'And if you need us, come and find us.' She strides towards the gate, looks back briefly and disappears around the corner.

The four of us go into the shed, stopping just inside the door.

'We're going to the Ramsay place first,' Kas says. 'That's where Hope is. After that, Swan's Marsh. We've got some gear stashed there. You can choose what to do then—come with us to the valley or join the No-landers.' Daymu and JT nod as she speaks.

As we step out of the shed there are distant gunshots.

We've got to go. Now.

The rain has eased to drizzle as we get to the main street. But Kas stops and looks. 'I'm going to find Yogi,' she says. 'I'll catch you up.'

'That's stupid, Kas.' I can't help myself. We haven't got time to stuff around looking for a horse.

'Think about it,' she says. 'When we get Hope we need to get her somewhere safe fast. And how long are you going to be able to walk with your arm as sore as it is?'

'There's a stable at the back of the pub,' JT says. 'I reckon that's your best bet.'

'Can you ride?' Kas asks.

'Shit, yeah,' he says, smiling. 'Been riding since I was five.'

'We'll wait here,' I say.

Daymu and I scout along the street a little and find a brick fence to hide behind. We don't have to wait long. Kas and JT come down the road at a canter. Kas is on Yogi, bareback, and JT is on a black beast of a thing the size of a draft horse. Daymu has to climb on from the top of the fence. Kas pulls me up by my good arm and we take off along the main street.

The town looks pretty rundown but it's nothing like Angowrie. The houses are still standing, and their roofs and windows are all intact. We follow the road. It's the quickest way to the edge of town and, right now, speed is everything. There'll be guards at the Ramsay place and who's to say they're not, right now, heading in our direction.

I hang on with one arm around Kas's waist, trying not to knock the wound. The shooting pain has changed to a constant ache, but the cream has eased some of the burning.

The buildings start to thin out. After a few minutes, we see the high metal poles of the railway line and, down the slope to our left, the deserted station. On our right, a driveway lined by an overgrown cypress hedge winds its way up the side of a hill. A milk-container letterbox hangs by the gate. We can just read the faded red paint on the side: *Ramsay.*

The hedge gives us good cover until the house comes into view. It's a red brick, double-storey place that looks like a big doll's house. There's an open area in front with no cover but there are trees on each side.

We tie up the horses. 'We'll split up, here,' Kas says, 'Finn and me to the right, you two to the left. Remember, JT, you're the only one who's armed. If this turns ugly, we'll be relying on you.'

We make our way up the side of the house. All the curtains are drawn, but French doors at the back are open and we hear voices inside. Before we can move, a man steps outside and sits down at a table on the patio. He rests a shotgun in front of him and begins to roll a cigarette.

I haven't seen anyone smoking in years. A girl, no older than me, walks out to join him. She sits in his lap and puts her arms around his neck.

'Sylvia,' Kas whispers.

The Wilder lights a match, draws on the cigarette and hands it to the girl.

'I'm so sick of this,' she says, leaning in and resting her head on the man's shoulder. He's younger than most Wilders, late twenties, maybe. He has a round face and a wispy beard. Sylvia's the best-fed Siley I've ever seen. She's bordering on fat.

'Me too,' the Wilder says. He slides his hands up under her top.

JT stands up behind them, his rifle raised. The Wilder tries to push Sylvia off his lap and grab his shotgun, but Daymu is too quick for him. She grabs his gun and steps back.

Kas and me run up onto the patio.

'What the...?' the Wilder says.

'Where's the baby?' Daymu demands, using the Wilder's shotgun to nudge Sylvia.

'The baby's Ramage's,' Sylvia says.

Kas has no interest in the argument. She walks into the house and her footsteps echo on the wooden floor.

The Wilder slowly picks up the cigarette and draws on it heavily. Smoke streams from his nostrils as he speaks. 'And what d'you think Ramage is going to do when he finds out you've taken her?'

Kas walks back out onto the patio, carrying a baby. Tears fill her eyes.

'Hope,' she says.

19

Hope's skin is dark and she has thick, black hair. She grabs Kas's finger in her little fist.

'What do you feed her?' Kas asks Sylvia.

Sylvia is reluctant to answer, but eventually she says, 'We found formula in a few of the houses in town, the ones that had lost babies to the virus. But the last couple of weeks we've tried stewed fruit and mashed veggies. We're nearly out of formula.'

The Wilder seems unfussed, cocky even. He leans back in his chair and scratches his beard. 'How are you going to look after a baby? You've got no idea.'

'Ramage will kill us,' Sylvia says, her voice frantic. 'You

don't know what he's like.'

'I reckon I've got a fair idea,' JT replies. He pulls his shirt-sleeve up to show the branded 'R' on his forearm. 'Now tell us what's been going on in Longley.'

The Wilder looks wary but Sylvia squeezes his arm. 'Tell them, Col,' she says.

'You probably know most of it,' Col begins. 'There's been a rebellion at the valley farm. It was bad enough when Ramage heard Rat was dead, but he went crazy when he heard you'd killed him,' he says, looking at Kas.

'How many men did he take with him?' Daymu asks.

Col shakes his head. He's not going to answer. But Daymu points the shotgun at his head. 'All he could spare,' he says, finally. 'He left a new bloke, Tusker, in charge. Complete bastard, dangerous.'

None of us says anything.

'Do you have food?' Daymu asks.

I'm keen to get moving but my stomach is empty. Hunger's already slowing us down. And who knows when we'll eat again.

Sylvia leads us inside. Col looks pissed off, now. JT keeps the rifle levelled at his back.

'Most of the food grown on the farms comes back to Longley,' Sylvia says. 'The farmers get the dregs. Ramage's got everyone under his control. No one's stood up to him until now. You've heard about the Sileys gone feral?'

'Not sure feral's the right word,' Daymu snaps. 'They're fighting back, that's all.'

'They've killed Wilders, stolen stock, burnt crops,' Col says.

'Ramage'll crush them once he's dealt with the upstarts in the valley.'

'Don't underestimate them,' Kas says.

There are eggs to eat, and stale bread. Then Sylvia drops four chops into the frying pan. The smell of them sends my stomach into a spin.

'Why are you doing this,' JT asks. 'Food is precious.' He's suspicious, smelling every forkful before putting it in his mouth.

'I'm a Siley,' Sylvia answers. 'It's been easier out here than at the feedstore, but I'm still a slave.'

'We need clothes,' Daymu says, hitching her shorts up.

'You'll find some upstairs,' Sylvia says.

Kas hands Hope to me, then she goes upstairs with Daymu. Hope is heavier than I thought she'd be. I hold her on my hip with my good arm and her hands reach for my face. She has Rose's eyes—deep brown and almond-shaped.

There's something I've wondered, ever since Ramage first chased Rose into Angowrie. 'I don't get you Wilders,' I tell Col. 'You must've been ordinary people before the virus, farmers, mechanics, teachers. How did you end up falling in with Ramage?'

'Don't judge us all the same, kid. When Ramage took over, most of us had no choice. It was follow him or end up like Ken Butler, dragged from here to Swan's Marsh behind a trail bike.'

I'm shocked to hear that name again. 'You knew Ken Butler?'

'I used to farm down near Nelson. I knew Ken since I was a kid.'

'But you still followed Ramage. Why?'

'Like I said, no choice. There are others like me, too. Blokes just waiting for their chance. But somehow Ramage always manages to find another animal, like Fenton or Wilson, blokes who'll kill just for the fun of it.'

'Wilson and Fenton won't be killing anyone anymore, ever.'

'Yeah, I heard that. Whoever it was that shot them, I'd like to pat them on the back.'

Kas and Daymu come down wearing jeans and warm shirts. They carry jackets and a bag of nappies.

'There's even undies!' Kas says, excited.

I hand Hope to Kas, and JT and I head up to find clothes for ourselves. There's a wardrobe full of them: long work pants, singlets, T-shirts and jumpers. I can't believe our luck.

When we're back in the kitchen, Sylvia explains. 'Ramsay ran one of the biggest farms in the district. He had eight kids. They all went in the first wave of the virus. No one realised the place was empty for months.'

The chops are cooked and she forks them out onto plates, along with big dollops of mashed potato.

'Ramage keeps us well stocked,' she says.

After we've eaten, Sylvia shows us how to change Hope's nappy. There's nothing tender in the way she holds her. I get the feeling she's happy to hand over the responsibility, even if it means Ramage will be as mad as hell.

She puts some mashed food in a couple of containers. 'Just little spoonfuls at a time,' she says. 'She'll cry if she gets an upset tummy.' Kas listens carefully and asks lots of questions, but she looks more and more worried. We never really thought about how we'd look after a four-month-old. The sooner we can get her to Stella the better, though we've got no idea what we'll find when we get back to the valley.

Sylvia goes to a cupboard and pulls out a funny-looking harness.

'It's a papoose,' she says, showing Kas how to put it on. 'You can carry the baby in the front when you walk.'

'Or ride,' Kas says.

JT and I take Col out to a shed in the yard, and lock him in. Sylvia's not a threat—she can't wait to get away, with or without Col.

Daymu has found a couple of saddlebags in the barn. The leather is cracked and dry, but they'll do the job.

Finally we bring the horses around the front. Kas climbs carefully onto Yogi's back, with Hope strapped in the papoose. I struggle up behind—my arm is almost numb by now. JT and Daymu mount the big black horse. He looks like a plough horse, with a wide arse and shaggy mane.

'Try to keep up,' Kas says, smiling.

'Don't worry about Black Bess, here,' JT says.

'Black Bess? Black Bus, more likely.'

Once we're out on the road the jokes drop away. We have to get moving but we don't want to make targets of ourselves.

'I say we skirt around Longley and find the road to Swan's Marsh,' Kas says. 'If any Wilders have followed the No-landers, they'll be ahead of us. We'll have to be alert.'

'We don't want to spend a night out in the open with Hope,'

I say. She's already unsettled with all the movement.

The land rises into patchy forest above the town. We stay clear of the buildings on the outskirts, then turn south and gain cover in the trees. The farms here are still being worked and there are gates and fences that slow our progress. From the tree line we get a good view of the town. We don't see anyone down there, but we've got to assume Tusker and the others at the feedstore will free themselves eventually, so we kick the horses into action.

Kas rides more upright, one hand on the reins and the other steadying Hope in the papoose. I loop my right arm around her waist and sit on the saddlebag straps to keep them in place. We don't get past a steady canter, and JT and Daymu keep up pretty easily. The rain has cleared and the afternoon sun slants through the trees.

We reach the top of a small ridge and see the road to Swan's Marsh winding through the foothills. I have a quick look back at Longley, hoping it's the last time I ever lay eyes on the place, then lean into Kas as she urges Yogi on. We stop a good distance from the road and ride parallel to it, even though it makes the going slower.

Kas tries to soothe Hope by talking to her quietly. Her voice takes on the rhythm of Yogi's canter. After a while, Hope nods off and Kas kicks Yogi to quicken his pace. JT is right behind us. Black Bess may be bit slower but I reckon she's bred tough. Daymu, though, looks as though she's spent about as much time on a horse as I have. She hangs on tight around JT's waist, her face turned and pressed against his back.

By the time the sun is low in the west, the bridge over the creek leading to the No-landers' farm comes into view. Straightaway it doesn't feel right. There's something on the bridge—maybe the Wilders are guarding it. Fifty metres above it we dismount and pull the horses back up into the trees. JT and I agree to check it out, while Kas tries to keep Hope quiet. There's not a breath of wind—any sound will carry for miles.

There's not much cover between us and the bridge so we drop down to the creek and make our way along its bank, keeping low and out of sight. We run the last ten metres to get under the bridge then sit and listen. Nothing.

Edging our way up the side we see two Wilders lying face down. Blood has pooled under them and filled cracks in the bitumen. I climb over the railing and nudge them with my boot. Neither one moves. My stomach heaves and I dry-retch. JT turns away, taking deep breaths.

We whistle for Kas and Daymu to come down.

They bring the horses onto the bridge and JT kneels and examines the bodies, one hand over his mouth.

'Shot in the back of the head,' he says.

'What?'

'Look at the way they've fallen—face first,' he says. 'I reckon they were on their knees.'

'Executed?' Daymu says, disbelief in her voice. 'But who'd do that?'

'There were lots of No-landers with guns,' JT says.

This is such a long way from anything I could have imagined when me and Rowdy were living down in Angowrie on our own. How did I end up in the middle of this?

There's only an hour of light left. We have to get to the valley quickly, but if we keep going today we'll only make it to the crossroad near Swan's Marsh, before it gets too dark to travel.

'I think we should find the No-landers' farm,' Kas says, lifting Hope out of the papoose and sliding her onto her hip. 'Stay the night there and ride for the valley tomorrow.'

'It's probably the best option,' Daymu says.

I know it's the logical thing to do, but the sight of the two bodies on the bridge stirs something in my gut—a gnawing feeling that seems to combine with the ache in my arm and put everything out of balance.

20

We roll the Wilders off the bridge and hide their bodies under a couple of branches. Then we follow the river up into the hills on the south side of the road. After half an hour of weaving the horses through stands of stringybarks and low-hanging sheoaks, the trees thin out into a clearing of rough paddocks. This valley looks lush but poorly tended, narrower than Harry and Stella's, with open country leading to the main range. Up there, a fire tower sticks out above the forest tops.

We barely make it out of the trees before No-landers appear on either side of us. They recognise us straightaway and two of them lead us on, while the others melt back into the bush.

Over the next small rise we see a farmhouse surrounded by a cluster of sheds. One of the No-landers whistles loudly and people come out into the yard. As we get closer there's a gathering of maybe twenty people—No-landers and feedstore kids. The place is shabby, the paddocks overrun with thistles and the buildings falling down. We've seen a few cattle on the way in but no other stock.

Danka welcomes us and helps Kas down off Yogi. She looks inside the papoose and smiles. 'This must be Hope,' she says.

'She's hungry,' Kas says, getting straight down to business.

Danka leads us to the biggest shed, which is divided into a hay barn and an open space that must have been used for farm machinery. It stinks of diesel.

Kas and I sit on a couple of hay bales to feed Hope. She squirms and turns her head away but eventually Kas gets her to eat some of the mashed vegetables. When she won't take anymore, I walk around the shed with her, rubbing her back and listening to her little burps.

Kas watches. 'You'd make a good dad,' she says, smiling.

'Yeah. Think I'd prefer to be her brother.'

We change her nappy, and Kas goes looking for a place for her to sleep.

I walk outside to find JT and Daymu. I've still got the image of the executed Wilders in my head. If the No-landers are responsible, they'll have to be prepared for a full-scale assault from the Wilders. It's something I don't want any part of; I'm not here to get involved in a war and I'm guessing a lot of the feedstore kids feel the same way. They're mostly all younger than the No-landers, and the ones here look no less afraid now than they did back in Longley.

Tahir and Gabriel meet us on the porch and take us inside the house. It's dark, the low eaves cutting out most of the natural light. A lamp burns on the table, where a map is opened out. There are pen marks, arrows fanning out from what I guess is the valley we're in.

We all sit at the table. Tahir and Gabriel are quiet. I get the feeling we're not a hundred per cent welcome.

'I thought you were heading back to help your friends?' Tahir says. His face is expressionless and I can't read his tone.

'We are,' I say. 'But we didn't want to spend the night in the open.'

'Are you sure you weren't followed?' Gabriel says.

Daymu and JT look at me. We are all thinking the same thing. 'The only Wilders we saw were dead,' I say. 'They'd been shot in the back of the head.'

Tahir's voice is hard, his jaw pushed out towards us. 'Sometimes these things are necessary in war,' he says.

'Are we at war, now?' Daymu asks.

'It's not one we started,' Tahir says, 'but it's one we are prepared to fight.'

'Fight with what?' JT's hands curl into fists and he rubs them on the table.

'There are more of us, now. And we have weapons,' Gabriel says.

'More? You mean the feedstore kids?' JT says. 'They're not fighters.'

'If they want to eat, they will fight,' Tahir says. He wears a singlet and I see the tattoos run all the way down onto his chest.

'And what if they don't want to fight?'

Tahir takes his time to answer. 'They can leave,' he says.

'And go where?' I ask.

'Where they go is not our responsibility.'

'You led them here with the promise of freedom and food,' I say.

'And I said they would have to fight,' he replies.

Daymu shakes her head. 'Even if they do fight, how will you feed them? I don't see any crops, there's hardly any stock and you've got fifteen extra mouths to feed.'

'A hunting party is going out tonight. Tomorrow we will feast.'

Tahir pushes his shoulders back. His stare is cold and his lip curls as he speaks. 'You think you can keep running and hiding from men like Ramage? You know nothing of the world. You know nothing of war. You were not born into it.'

'Most Sileys came here to escape from war,' Daymu shoots back.

'Yes, but it's followed you, hasn't it,' Tahir says. 'It is the way of men.' He folds his arms across his chest, challenging us to argue with him.

'We just want to sleep in the shed tonight,' I say, 'then we'll go.'

He dismisses us with a wave of his hand. 'One night,' he says. 'And tomorrow you leave.'

Back in the shed, Kas is walking around with Hope, trying to get her to sleep. Danka sits on a hay bale.

'What did they say?' Kas asks.

I fill her in on our conversation with Gabriel and Tahir.

'And the Wilders on the bridge?' Kas asks.

'Just what we thought,' JT says. 'Executed.'

'I don't like it here,' Daymu says. 'It doesn't feel right.'

I'm thinking of Harry and the farmers in the valley, fighting a war of their own. 'If Ramage gets back to Longley in one piece, or if Tusker gets wind of where we're hiding, we'll be caught in the middle. We have to get away.'

'We?' Danka says. 'Who's we?'

It's a question I don't want to answer. I'm not just thinking of our safety—food is going to be a huge problem no matter what happens. I look to Kas but she stays quiet.

Danka stands her ground. 'We're all in this,' she says. 'I'm responsible for the kids we brought here. We should work this out together.'

'Any ideas?' I ask.

'What's it like down on the coast?' JT asks.

This is where I was afraid the discussion would lead. Kas and me could survive in Angowrie. We could hunt and fish and grow some food of our own. But we couldn't support many more.

'What are you thinking?' Kas asks JT.

'Well,' he says, 'I know you two want to go back to the valley. But what are you planning after that? Are you going to stay there?'

'We haven't decided,' Kas says. 'We don't even know if the

valley people will still be there. But we need Stella to help look after Hope.'

'I'll be going back to the coast, regardless,' I say, and I feel Kas's gaze bore into me.

Daymu opens the saddlebags and spreads the food on a hay bale over by the door. There's bread, dried meat, fruit and cold potatoes. Danka's eyes widen. 'Where did this come from?' she asks.

But before we can start eating, the feedstore kids make their way into the shed.

Daymu doesn't hesitate. She breaks the bread up into small portions and cuts apples into quarters. She does the same with the potatoes and then slices the meat into thin strips.

I count fourteen of us. We only get a few mouthfuls each. The kids shove the food into their mouths and chew loudly, sucking the last taste of grease off their fingers. They're a ragged lot, and there's a smell to them that says they haven't washed in ages.

The food disappears quickly, and Kas and I find a spot in the hay to bed down. Kas places Hope between us and we snuggle around her.

'What'd you think?' Kas whispers.

'I dunno. It kinda feels like we're not on our own anymore.'

'Food,' she says. 'That's the problem.'

'Yeah, you saw how hungry they are.'

'If we had guns we could hunt, not have to rely on trapping rabbits.'

'I know. But we'd run out of ammunition before too long.'

'The No-landers have ammo.'

'For their war with the Wilders, not for us.'

'They can't feed everyone that's followed them here. We could bargain with them.'

'How?'

'We'll take the kids that don't want to stay here. They must know they're not fighters.'

'And do what with them?'

'JT, Daymu and Danka can lead them to the coast, while we head for the valley.'

'I don't know if the No-landers are in the mood to bargain. Tahir doesn't trust us.'

'It's a good deal for him. He won't have to feed the kids.'

'We'll talk to the others in the morning,' I say.

I hardly get the words out before we hear JT say, 'Good idea.' He's in the next stall and has heard everything.

'It's okay,' Daymu says. 'We're with you.'

'Me too,' Danka's voice comes from the other side.

I have a broken sleep. My arm aches and Hope cries half a dozen times during the night. Kas and I take it in turns to walk her around the shed in the dark. I wake before dawn to see Kas holding Hope on her shoulder. She's rubbing her back and singing softly.

'How is she?' I ask.

'Hungry.'

'Like the rest of us.'

Kas passes Hope to me, then sits down in the hay.

'I think we should pack up and get out of here,' she says. 'Now.'

'What's the rush?' I say.

Daymu sticks her head over the top of the bales. JT follows.

'I've been thinking about something all night,' Kas says. 'Something that doesn't make sense.'

Daymu and JT come in and sit down. Danka has stirred too. She walks over and squats in front of us.

'What?' I say.

'You know when we met Tahir and Gabriel near Pinchgut Junction and you said something didn't add up?'

'Yeah,' I say.

'They said they were looking for Rose to lead them,' Kas explains. 'But, do they seem like a group that needs a leader to you? They answer to no one.'

'Why were they looking for Rose then?'

'Maybe,' she pauses. 'Maybe for the same reason Tusker wanted to keep me in the valley last autumn. To bargain—'

'With Ramage?'

'It makes sense, doesn't it?' she says. 'They'd have heard how much Ramage wanted to find Rose. And they obviously didn't know she'd died.'

'All right,' I say, 'but why's that a problem now?'

'Don't you see?' Kas says. 'Hope is Rose's baby. The No-landers don't know that yet, but if they find out—'

'They'll want to keep her,' Daymu says.

JT and Daymu look at each other. JT nods. 'We'll help you,' he says. 'If any of the kids want to stay with the No-landers, they can, but the ones that don't, we'll take them to the coast.'

'That'll be a tough trip,' I say. 'Some of the kids mightn't be up to it.'

'I know,' JT says, 'but if the only other option is going to war, it's worth a try.'

'You'll have to steal some ammo,' Kas says. 'Somehow everyone who makes it to the coast has to be fed.'

Kas glances at me as she speaks, and I know what she's thinking. She's not sure she'll be going back to the coast herself.

Morning light filters into the barn as Kas throws the saddlebags over Yogi. JT has offered to lend us Black Bess, but Kas says she hasn't got time to escape and teach me how to ride. As for me, I'm just relieved.

'It's a pity,' JT says, smiling. 'I would've liked to see surfer boy trying to ride Bess.' I'm starting to like his dry sense of humour. Of all the people we've met since leaving Angowrie, he's the one most like me. More importantly, he's given us his rifle to take with us.

Some of the feedstore kids are stirring by the time we're ready to go.

Kas and I have fed Hope and now we strap her into the papoose. We say our goodbyes quickly, wanting to get going before the remaining No-landers are up. As far as we know, the hunting party hasn't returned yet.

We climb onto Yogi and Kas nudges him towards the door of the shed. She looks over her shoulder at our three friends. 'Take care,' she says.

The morning is cool and a mist hugs the creek where it winds through the valley. The farm looks deserted. We're halfway across the yard when the door of the house flies open and Tahir steps out, a rifle in his hands. 'Stop!' he yells.

I feel Kas flinch.

'Hang on,' she whispers.

Tahir walks at a fast pace towards us. At the same time Danka leads the kids out of the shed. Flanked by JT and Daymu they place themselves between Tahir and us.

'What's going on?' Tahir says, his voice loud, angry.

Kas wheels Yogi around to face Tahir. 'We're leaving,' she says.

'I decide who leaves, and when,' Tahir says.

'You said we should leave in the morning,' I say. 'And now we are.'

He looks around for support but the rest of No-landers are with the hunting party. 'What's the hurry?' he says.

A girl I haven't seen before, short with a shock of black curls, steps out of the house.

'Vashti!' Kas says, under her breath.

'The baby,' she calls to Tahir. 'The baby belongs to Ramage. It's not Kas's, it's her sister's.'

Tahir spins back around and begins waving the rifle in the air. 'You've lied to me, again,' he snarls. 'Now hand me the child.' He raises the gun to his shoulder and aims at us.

At the same moment the kids press in closer to him, blocking his aim. When Tahir shoots into the air they duck but they come straight back up to protect us.

Kas digs her heals into Yogi's flanks. His weight goes onto

his back legs and I have to grab Kas to stop from falling as he lurches forward. Then we're off and out the gate, Kas leaning into Yogi's mane. 'Come on, boy,' she urges.

Hope's high-pitched wail rises above the sound of Yogi's pounding hoofs.

The road turns away from the creek, a row of trees hiding us from the house. I chance a look back but I don't think anyone is coming after us. I hope JT and the others are okay.

Kas pulls Yogi back to a canter. The road stretches out ahead of us to the mouth of the valley. 'If there's anyone out here, if they try to stop us, play it cool,' Kas says.

Before long we're out of the paddocks and into the trees. Hope settles with the slower movement. Where the track takes a dogleg, two No-landers appear from the bush on either side of us. Both have guns. I recognise them from the raid on the feed-store, Afa and Kaylo. They are big boys, thickset and muscled under their dirty clothes.

'We heard a shot,' Afa says. 'What's happening back there?'

Kas is ready for them. 'Must have been the hunting party,' she says, keeping her voice casual. 'There'll be a feast tonight.'

Afa smiles but Kaylo moves closer, taking hold of Yogi's bridle. 'You're leaving,' he says, suspicious.

'We just needed shelter for the night,' I say. 'For the baby.'

He looks up at me. 'But you're safe in the valley.'

'We've got to get the baby to its mother,' Kas says, pulling gently on the rein to try to break Kaylo's grip. 'Over past Swan's Marsh.'

'It's dangerous country out there,' he says.

Kas doesn't show a hint of nervousness, but my heart is pounding in my chest. 'We know the country pretty well,' she says, smiling. 'Better than any No-Lander.'

Afa laughs but Kaylo isn't buying it. He's about to speak again when Kas butts in. 'Tahir wants you to head back to the farmhouse. Something about helping with the hunt,' she says.

This doesn't go down well with Kaylo. He scowls. 'Who elected Tahir leader, anyway,' he says to Afa.

'Not my business,' Kas says, 'but he wasn't in a good mood so I reckon you'd better do what he says.'

'Let him wait,' Kaylo says, spitting on the ground.

'Do what you like,' Kas says, giving Yogi a little kick. We move off slowly, half expecting them to call us to stop but all we hear is arguing. When we get around the next turn in the track, Kas urges Yogi into a canter.

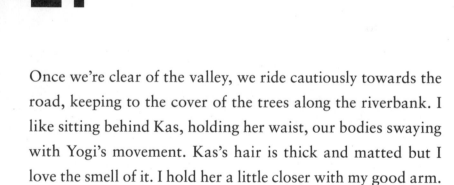

21

Once we're clear of the valley, we ride cautiously towards the road, keeping to the cover of the trees along the riverbank. I like sitting behind Kas, holding her waist, our bodies swaying with Yogi's movement. Kas's hair is thick and matted but I love the smell of it. I hold her a little closer with my good arm.

'You right back there?' she says, turning and smiling.

'Just getting comfortable.'

Hope wriggles in the papoose. 'She'll be hungry again, soon,' Kas says.

'Let's see if we can get to the crossroad where the packs are. We can feed her there and keep an eye on the road at the same time,' I say.

We see the bridge first, then the road winding off in both directions—left to Longley and right to Swan's Marsh. As we get closer, I make out the bodies of the two Wilders. We can't avoid going past them. They throw my mind back to the Wilder I found with the knife in his chest in the paddock at Angowrie, last autumn. His skin had the same horrible blue tinge.

We pass them quickly, and I run up the bank to check the road. It looks clear so I whistle to Kas. We cross over and I get back on Yogi in the paddock on the other side. It's a couple of hundred metres to the safety of the trees up the slope to the north. From here, we can ride parallel to the road until we reach the crossroad.

The sun is well up now. I can feel it prickling the back of my neck. If we weren't in such a dangerous place we could take our time and enjoy the morning. It's beautiful out here. The hills roll away to the east, and the leaning fence posts along the road look like crooked teeth. Up higher the tips of the grey gums outline the ridge against the deep blue of the sky.

When Hope begins to cry, Kas takes the reins in one hand and rubs her back with the other. 'It's okay, sweetie,' she says. 'Not long now.'

But it takes the best part of an hour to get to the junction where the road veers off towards the plains. Hope is crying constantly, but we keep moving, finally reaching the stand of wattles where we hid the packs.

We dismount quickly and Kas gives Hope the last of the mashed veggies. From up here we can see smoke rising from the chimney of the general store in Swan's Marsh. I'm grateful we don't need to go that way. The last thing we need is to meet the Monahans again, though I'm guessing after the way Tusker treated them, they might be rethinking their support for Ramage.

I carefully unwind the bandage on my arm. The swelling has eased a little but the skin is still raw and the branded 'R' rises black and sore. I dab more cream onto it and Kas helps redo the bandage.

The packs are where we left them. I open two cans of beans and we sit back against a fallen log to eat. Kas passes Hope to me. Her little body is warm against my shoulder.

Kas pauses between mouthfuls of beans. 'We could never look after her on our own,' she says. 'She's so dependent. But…'

'What?'

She pulls her hair back with one hand and turns to look at me. 'There's something you should know.'

'What?'

Her eyes fix on some object in the distance. 'I'm not ready to be her mother, but I don't think I can leave her. I'll have to stay in the valley,' she says.

Something freezes inside me.

She pauses, then adds, 'Will you stay with me?'

Just the possibility of not going back to the coast throws my mind into a spin. I can't find the words to respond. All I want is to be with Kas, but Angowrie is where I belong. And what if JT and Daymu arrive and we're not there?

'Forget it,' she says, her voice short. 'You're so—'

'So what?'

'So selfish.'

This stings somewhere deep. 'That's bullshit, and you know it. Wasn't it me who helped Rose? Me who went searching for you? Me who led us back to Angowrie? How's that selfish?'

Kas takes Hope and puts her into the papoose. She walks off to get Yogi, leaving me standing there. I fuss about with the packs, stuffing food into saddlebags, trying not to look at her.

'Shit!' Kas's voice is low, urgent. She's pointing to the road.

A group of men is moving towards Swan's Marsh. I count six of them. They're a hundred metres from us, but I'm sure the leader is Tusker from the way he walks, his eyes scanning right and left, a rifle in his hands.

Kas takes Yogi's bridle and pulls him back behind some low-hanging branches. I drop to the ground, suddenly short of breath. When I look over the top, they've passed us, the stragglers hurrying to keep up with Tusker.

'They're on a mission,' Kas says. 'We gotta move.'

We wait until the Wilders fall out of sight behind a small rise. I stash the packs back under the logs and we hurry up the hill to the road. Yogi is fidgety, feeling the urgency in Kas. We mount quickly and Kas soon has Yogi at a fast canter, putting distance between us and the Wilders. We stick to the road for a good ten minutes before veering back up into the trees, all the while making our way north—away from one sort of danger, and heading into another.

It's strange holding onto Kas now. Her body tenses against my grip. She pushes Yogi harder than she needs to, like she wants to take her anger out in the riding.

Yogi is sweating. But Kas keeps urging him on, weaving through the trees. Branches swat at me when she ducks unexpectedly and we come close enough to some of the trunks for me to feel the bark brush against my legs. My arm aches with all the swaying. I swear Kas is trying to knock me off.

Finally, she slows Yogi to a trot, then a walk. I take my chance and slide off, happy to feel the ground under my feet. Yogi is blowing hard and throws his head from side to side.

'Jesus, Kas, what're you trying to do? Kill us?'

She doesn't answer but leans forward and pats Yogi's sweat-drenched neck. 'It's okay, boy,' she says, 'we can take it easy for a while.'

There's a thick silence between us now. We push on through the bush, Kas ahead and me walking behind. The land dips away to a small stream where she dismounts to let Yogi drink.

'I should have killed him when I had the chance,' Kas says, but I can't tell if she's talking to me or to herself.

'Tusker?'

She doesn't answer.

When we get moving again, Kas walks, leading Yogi to give him a rest. The argument we had swirls around in my head. I hate it when we're not talking to each other. I quicken my pace and come up next to her.

'Hey,' I say.

She keeps walking.

I touch her on the shoulder and she stops, dropping her head so her hair hides her face. 'I can't work you out,' she says.

'What d'you mean?'

'One minute I think you want to be with me, have me close. And the next minute you don't even answer my question. What am I supposed to think, Finn?'

'I didn't know what to say. You didn't give me a chance.'

'Okay, so here's your chance,' she says, dragging the hair back off her face.

'I do want to be with you. I just—'

'Just what?'

'I have to think.'

'Think about what? We promised Rose we'd look after Hope. You can't make a promise like that and then just dump it because it gets difficult. Here's the deal, Finn: you're either all in or all out. There's no halfway.'

The look on her face breaks me open. It's a mixture of anger and defiance and need. I feel like shit, like all I do is let her down. 'I'm sorry,' I say.

'I don't want you to be sorry, I want to know whether you're in or you're out?'

'I'm in,' I say, quietly at first, but then louder, 'I'm in.'

'All the way?' she demands.

'All the way,' I say.

We mostly travel up through the trees, but sometimes lower down in the open country too, where Yogi can stretch out and we can really cover some ground. Hope cries a lot of the time. Eventually, the two windmills come into sight, standing out on the plain catching the glow of the setting sun. When they line up we turn into the bush and begin the climb to the valley entrance.

We move slowly now, taking care not to turn any corner in the track without checking what's beyond it. Hope is quiet for the time being but it's hard to hide Yogi's bulk, so if we come across anyone they're going to spot us.

It's not quite dark when the track drops closer to the river. This is where we last saw Steb and Vic when we left the valley. The grove of trees is quiet. No guards meet us as we push through to where the land opens out.

What I do see, are clear tyre tracks from a trail bike. Ramage is somewhere in the valley.

'No guards here at the entrance—that's strange,' I say.

'They might've followed the Wilders to the farm, attacked them from behind.'

'Maybe. We need to get as close as we can and try to figure out what's happening.'

'I don't want to spend the night in the open. We're out of food for Hope and we won't be able to keep her warm enough.'

The night is clear but the wind is up, making it hard for us to hear anyone approaching. A quarter-moon nudges over the ridge and provides enough light for us to make our way along the gravel road. We both lean forward, straining to hear anything coming towards us.

Then Kas pulls Yogi to a halt. We're completely exposed here. If anyone comes, we'll have nowhere to hide.

'What is it?' I whisper.

'Shh.'

I can't hear anything other than Yogi's breath and my own heart pounding in my ears. Until I pick it up—the unmistakable sound of a motor.

A trail bike.

22

'Ride!' I yell at Kas as I jump off Yogi, my feet slipping on the muddy track.

Kas circles me, pulling hard on the reins, uncertain.

'Go,' I say. 'I've got this.'

But she stays.

There's something odd about the sound of the trail bike; the motor is labouring. There's a small rise twenty metres ahead of us blocking our view. The bike is misfiring now.

Finally, it reaches the top of the hill and splutters to a stop.

There's hardly any sound, just the wind and the pinging of the motor as it cools. The rider is silhouetted against the sky, standing astride the bike as he leans forward and peers into the gloom.

'Look after Hope,' I whisper, standing in the middle of the track with the rifle in my hands.

The bike rolls a few metres down the incline and stops. Yogi's snorting makes the rider sit up.

Then, I hear a scared and aching voice. 'Help.'

It's Willow. She's on the bike, in front of the rider.

Whoever it is on the bike with her, he's breathing heavily, in pain. He raises one arm until the outline of a handgun is clear against the sky. When he speaks his voice is low. 'Let me pass.'

It's Ramage.

'He's shot,' Willow says, her voice cracking.

Ramage lifts his head. 'You fuckin' kids,' he spits.

He has an arm tight around Willow's neck.

'Now, let me pass,' Ramage says, 'or I'll....'

'Enough,' Kas yells, the sharpness of her voice sending Yogi skittering sideways. She pulls him back and holds her ground.

Willow lets out a wail that seems to fill the valley. 'He killed my dad,' she screams. 'He killed my dad.'

It feels like a rock has hit me in the chest. *Harry.*

Ramage loses his balance and lurches to the side, scrambling to get a grip as the weight of Willow and the bike begin to topple him. He manages to get his footing, staggering away from the bike and dragging Willow with him. But as soon as she feels the ground under her feet, Willow pushes away and runs to Yogi and Kas.

Ramage is no more than ten metres from them. He's holding

his shoulder, but he manages to point the gun at Kas and Willow. And Hope.

I hear the click of the gun as he tries to fire. He checks it and raises it again.

Kas moves quickly, scooping Willow up with one arm before digging her heels into Yogi's flanks. 'Shoot him,' Kas yells. 'Shoot him.'

Yogi's hooves slip but he gets enough purchase to take off into the darkness, leaving Ramage and me alone.

Ramage steadies his gun, aiming at me now.

Another click.

I've been lucky a second time.

The rifle is heavy in my hands and it feels like my whole body is creased in some way. My arms are so tense I can hardly lift them. I plant my feet in the gravel and strain to bring the rifle to my shoulder.

But Ramage slumps back, falling into the grass and letting out a cry that could be pain or could be anger. I step towards him, close enough to see the gun has fallen from his hand. I kick it away and stand above him, the rifle aimed at his chest.

He clutches the wound on his shoulder.

The moon gives enough light for me to see Ramage's face. He looks older than I remember and, somehow, smaller. It's only four months since I held a knife at his throat in the hayshed paddock. How different would things be now if I'd killed him when I had the chance? Before he killed Harry.

I take a step away as he shifts his backside towards a large rock by the side of the track. He looks out across the paddocks, then back to me. 'What's your name, boy? I never found out.' He talks like he's got stones in his mouth.

I'm standing in front of him, just out of reach.

'Finn.'

He groans. 'Finn? Like a fish?'

'I guess so.'

He shifts slightly, trying to find a more comfortable position. 'On the horse, that was Warda's sister?'

'Kas.'

'And the baby? Shauna?'

'Hope. Yeah, her too.' There's no point in lying to him.

'Hope,' he says. I'm not sure but I think he nods his head. He hauls himself up, pushing his shoulders back against the rock. 'You think I'm to blame for Warda dying, don't you?'

I don't say anything. It's too bizarre, this conversation.

'You've got it all wrong, kid. It wasn't me who killed Warda. It was you. You hid her from me when she needed proper care. She could have lived. But no, you had to play the hero.'

Anger rises in my chest. 'She hated you!' I scream. 'She never would have gone back to Longley.'

'She was sick. And I only wanted to look after her.' His voice trails off. 'I loved her,' he says.

It's the way adults argue, twisting everything until you almost believe they're right. I think back to the night Rose died, the way Ramage kissed her, mourned her.

But hate's like dirt that's worked its way into the creases of your skin. You can scrub as hard as you like but it's still there.

'Hunting her down when she was pregnant and injured, that was love, was it?' I say.

He moves again, wincing, but gathering his strength. 'You only heard one side of that story,' he says.

'It was enough.'

His eyes shift to my rifle and he changes tack. 'You're naïve, kid—that's your problem. You don't know how the world works. You've gotta take your opportunities. Surely your parents taught you that?'

Him mentioning Mum and Dad, people he never knew and who were nothing like him, flicks a switch in me somewhere. Why shouldn't I shoot him? I could kill him and no one would care, probably not even his own men. They seem to hate him almost as much as I do.

Ramage pushes his weight against the rock and climbs to his feet, all the time looking straight at me, smirking.

His voice comes low and harsh, 'Your arm,' he says, pointing at the bandage covering the burn. 'You're mine, now.'

I point to the ragged scar across the back of his hand where I cut him, that morning in the hayshed paddock. 'I reckon we're even,' I say.

He turns his back on me and walks towards the trail bike. But I'm ahead of him by a couple of metres and I place myself between him and the bike, my rifle raised.

'What are you going to do, kid? Kill me? You couldn't do it last time.'

This time the anger takes hold of my whole body. It comes from somewhere deep and it's about Mum and Dad and Ray and

Rose. And now Harry, too. All the shit things that happened to them, all the hurt and tears.

I squeeze the trigger. He cringes, bringing his hands up to cover his face.

'Jesus,' he yells and it's as though the force of the word pushes him backwards. Suddenly he's less sure of himself—not knowing whether I missed him deliberately or not.

Without taking his eyes off me, he picks up the trail bike and drags his leg over. 'This is it, boy,' he says. 'Your last chance.'

He pushes up and faces me, smiling now. 'See,' he says, snarling, 'this is why you'll never win. Mercy's a great quality, kid—but only if everyone's playing by the same rules.'

The motor rumbles into life, splutters and dies. He tries again and this time it takes. I hear the sound of the gear clicking into place. Ramage leans forward and the bike starts to move.

I bring the rifle to my shoulder. The metal trigger is cold against my finger.

I breathe in.

'You're wrong,' I yell, 'about everything.'

But for all the fear and hate and loathing, I can't squeeze the trigger. It's as though another larger, stronger hand covers mine and a voice I remember from years ago whispers in my ear saying, *this isn't us, this isn't us.*

And the trail bike is swallowed by the night.

23

'*Finn!*' Kas calls. I've walked a couple of hundred metres towards the farm and I'm still shaking. It takes me a few seconds to work out where her voice is coming from. 'You okay?' she says, nudging Yogi forward out of the dark. 'Did you shoot him?'

I try to speak but nothing comes out.

Willow slides off Yogi's back and runs to me, burying her face in my shirt, big sobs jerking her body. 'Dad,' she finally says, the word heaving out of her. 'There was a big fight. Dad got shot.'

Kas dismounts slowly, holding Hope in the papoose with

one arm. 'Wils,' she says, 'is it safe for us to go to the farm?'

Willow is struggling to speak. 'I don't know,' she says between sobs.

'How many Wilders are there?' Kas asks.

'I'm not sure. Lots. Some are dead.'

Kas doesn't say anything more. I give her a leg-up onto Yogi and she reaches her hand down to pull Willow up. I slide the rifle back over my shoulder. I walk behind them, my mind reliving the conversation with Ramage, my ears hearing nothing but the wind and my teeth grinding in my jaw. My anger spills into tears. I don't know if it's anger at Ramage, or anger at myself for not killing him.

As we get closer to the farm we push uphill to the west side of the valley, so we can keep Yogi out of sight and approach the buildings from behind. There are lamps burning in Harry and Stella's place but everything else is dark. With Yogi tied to a fence rail in the cattle yards we inch our way towards the back of the house. Willow sticks close, holding the back of my shirt.

Kas slips the papoose off and hands Hope to me. 'I'll go around the front and see if I can get a look in one of the windows,' she says.

Willow, Hope and I hide behind the wood stack and Kas disappears into the dark. Hope starts to wriggle and I'm worried she's going to cry. I hold her to me and rub her back. From here I can see the row of sheds over near Rachel's place and I make out shapes in the open ground of the yard. Bodies.

Then the back door opens and a lamp moves towards us.

'Willow?' Stella's voice cuts through the night.

I grab hold of Willow's arm and pull her back. But then a familiar shape comes towards us and Rowdy nearly bowls me over.

Kas calls out from the house. 'It's okay, Finn. Come in.'

I don't have a spare arm to pat Rowdy so I drop to my knees and let him lick my face. 'Hello, boy, did you miss me?'

Stella runs to Willow and hugs her.

'This is Hope,' I say, holding her up to Stella.

She lifts Hope out of the papoose and nuzzles her into her neck. 'Finn,' she says, 'it's Harry. Come inside.'

Harry is lying on his back on the kitchen table, three lamps hanging low from the ceiling above him. It looks like there's been a fight in the house—broken chairs, the dresser over-turned, and the front door is hanging off one hinge. Harry's chest is bare and Rachel is cleaning a wound just below his ribcage on the left side. The table is covered with blood.

I see his chest rise and fall. I wipe tears away and grip the back of a chair to steady myself. He's alive!

Stella stands with Willow at the end of the table, one hand on Harry's leg, the other clutching Hope to her chest. Kas takes Hope, who starts to cry. Rachel looks up with the sound and the lamplight catches her eyes. She nods her head towards Stella. *Help her,* she mouths.

'Stella,' Kas says, 'Hope hasn't eaten in hours and I need to change her. Wils, go and get the saddlebags. We need some nappies.'

Willow is grateful to have something to do, and Stella moves around the table, not taking her eyes off Harry.

'What can I do?' I ask Rachel.

'More warm water,' she says. The kitchen is a hive of activity, taps running, pots clanging on the stovetop and everyone trying not to bump into each other. 'We have to stem the bleeding and—' Rachel hesitates, 'I have to get the bullet out.'

Stella breathes in deeply. Rachel grabs my hand and pushes it on the cloth over the wound. 'Pressure. Here,' she says. Then she takes Stella by the shoulders and shakes her. 'Help me,' she says. 'We can save him.'

Stella lets go of the breath she's been holding and the energy seems to return to her body. 'Right,' she says.

Harry's body starts to jerk on the table. He's having a fit.

'Roll him onto his side,' Rachel says. 'He's choking.'

Harry's a big man. Even though his body is wasted from the winter, it takes two of us to push him onto his good side, leaving the wound on top. Blood and vomit spill from his mouth before his breathing becomes more regular again.

Rachel is supporting Harry's head. 'Towels,' she says, 'blankets, cushions, whatever you can find,' her voice strong, in command. 'We need to hold him in this position.'

Stella turns to the stove, opens the fire door and shoves more wood in. She sharpens a knife, drops it and a pair of tweezers into a pot of boiling water. When Willow returns with the saddlebags, she and Kas disappear into the bedroom with Hope.

Stella leans down and holds Harry's face in her hands. 'Don't you dare leave me, you hear? Don't you dare.' Her voice is soft though, gentle. She kisses his forehead and stands up.

'Now,' Rachel says, 'I need all hands on deck. If he wakes—and he probably will—you have to restrain him, keep him still.'

Kas and Willow come back into the kitchen. 'She's asleep,' Kas says before I can ask about Hope.

Willow's eyes are wide but she positions herself at her father's feet. We've rolled blankets along his side to support him. Stella holds his head while Kas and I are opposite each other, pushing our weight against him. Rachel drains the pot and waits until the knife is cool enough to use.

'Right,' she says. She opens the wound by rolling her thumbs either side of it, then alternates between wiping the blood away and pushing the knife deeper into the opening. Harry starts to convulse again, his body lifting and shaking. Willow cops a foot to her chest but she picks herself up off the floor and grabs him by the ankles again.

Rachel waits until Harry is still, then goes back to work. Kas and I are straining to hold him on the table, our heads almost touching as we lean in from each side.

I don't know how long it takes but it feels like hours of Harry coming alive with the pain, then falling back unconscious, only to start awake again. There's nothing delicate in what Rachel's doing, digging into the open wound looking for the bullet. Stella has her head turned away, and Willow presses her chest against her father's legs. There's a moment when Kas and I lock eyes. My strength is falling away and my branded arm is throbbing but everything in her eyes tells me I can't quit.

'Tweezers!' Rachel says. Two fingers of each hand are knuckle deep in the wound.

234

'Trace my right index finger down,' Rachel says to Kas, her voice amazingly calm.

Kas's hand shakes but she steadies herself and pushes in with the tweezers. 'I feel it!' she says.

'Take it slow. Slow,' Rachel says.

Finally Kas holds the little lump of metal up to the light. Rachel quickly puts pressure back on the wound before pushing small pieces of clean cloth in just below the skin. She looks up. 'I don't know what damage has been done inside,' she says. 'All we can do now is clean around it and stitch him up. The rest is in God's hands.'

Once she finishes the stitching we carry Harry into the bedroom and somehow manage to get him onto the bed. Stella and Willow stay with him while Rachel, Kas and I clean up the kitchen.

Rachel is exhausted. She sits down at the table and her head slumps onto her folded arms.

'Has he got a chance?' I ask her.

'The wound's on the left side—if it was on the right he'd be dead. But he's lost a lot of blood and the risk of infection is high. He's strong, though. And stubborn. As long as he's breathing, there's hope.'

'What happened?' Kas asks, 'when the Wilders came.'

Rachel sits back in her chair and hugs her arms to her chest. 'We waited for ages,' she begins. 'We started to think maybe they'd leave us alone—or it could be we just wanted to believe that.' A small smile crosses her lips then the frown returns to her face. 'They arrived yesterday, about twenty of them. Steb and Jack were guarding the valley entrance. They killed four or five of the Wilders, then took off into the bush and made their way back here. We heard the shots. Harry led a group out and they hid along the sides of the road: Will, Vic and Simmo. James and Kate took the young ones up towards the ridge at the back but Willow refused to go. She had her bow and arrows and she wanted to fight.'

Rachel smiles again. 'She's tough, that one.'

'Tell me something I don't know,' I say.

'The whole thing was so confused—gunshots, people yelling, screams in the night. We regrouped in the morning but Vic and Will were missing. Ramage arrived later, probably thinking it'd all be over and he'd just ride in and take control again. But the Wilders weren't organised at all. We reckon some of them took off when the fighting got tough. In the end, just half a dozen of them followed Ramage into the yard. He sat there on his trail bike, barking orders and telling us to show ourselves. Harry stepped out to confront him, Steb and Jack with him. It was a stand off until a couple of the Wilders panicked and started shooting. Ramage rode straight at Harry. Fired from close in, but Harry shot him first.'

Rachel stops and shakes her head. 'No one saw Willow out there. She shot one of the Wilders in the leg with an arrow before Ramage swung around and nearly ran over her. He grabbed her, dragged her onto his bike and took off.'

She looks at us, one after the other. 'Where did you find her?' she asks.

'We ran straight into them. Willow escaped.' I say.

'And Ramage?' Rachel looks at me with hope in her eyes.

'He was wounded.'

Kas doesn't say anything but I can see the question in her eyes.

'I couldn't do it,' I say. My face burns.

I get to my feet and walk to the washroom.

Kas follows me. We stand with our shoulders touching, washing the blood off our hands and arms.

'Don't blame yourself,' she says.

I can't look at her.

'I don't know what's going to happen,' she says, 'but I want to be with you, no matter what. I—'

'You what?'

'Nothing.'

'Kas?'

'Tonight, when we were holding Harry and I looked up at you, in the middle of all that I felt something so strong.'

'What?'

It comes out as hardly more than a whisper. 'I love you,' she says.

It's like a thousand strings that've been pulling tight across my chest suddenly let go and I can breathe again.

'I've never said that to anyone,' she says.

Everything that's happened today is spinning around in my head, but above all of it is Kas, right next to me, the smell of her hair, her breath on my skin.

And she loves me.

24

In the morning the house is quiet. I find Stella in the kitchen asleep at the table. Kas is with Harry. 'How is he?' I ask.

'Breathing,' she says.

'That's good, then.'

'Yeah, that's good.'

It's a relief to get out of the house after breakfast. Rowdy's not going to let me out of his sight. He limps into the sunshine and I get my first chance to have a good look at him. The wounds on his hip are healing well and he's put on some weight. He can't move like he used to but his eyes are bright and his tail hasn't stopped wagging all morning.

The bodies I saw in the yard last night have been moved, and it doesn't take me long to find Jack out in the paddock, digging more graves.

'Need a hand?' I say, approaching him from behind.

He points at a long-handled shovel on the ground. 'Go your hardest,' he says.

Rowdy watches us work.

'How's Harry?' Jack asks, as I start to dig.

'Alive.'

'Rachel herded us all out last night, said there were too many people around for her to think.'

'She operated on him.'

'Shit! And he's still alive? Make sure she doesn't feed him anything she cooks, that'll finish him off for sure.'

I can never tell when Jack's taking the piss. But this time he smiles and nudges me with his shovel handle. 'He's as tough as a Mallee bull, Finn. He'll make it.'

'Who are we burying?' I ask.

He stops and looks towards the back of the shearing shed, where bodies are laid out on the ground, each covered with a sheet of black plastic. 'Wilders,' he says, spitting the word out. 'They don't deserve a decent burial but what else are we going to do with them?'

'Rachel said Vic and Will are missing.'

'We haven't seen them since yesterday morning. We're hoping they're chasing the Wilders that took off into the bush.' He strikes his shovel hard into the wet earth and throws the soil on a heap behind him.

'No one else was hurt though, no one from the valley?' I say.

'Lots of cuts and bruises but other than that we escaped okay. What about you?' he says, looking at the bandage on my arm.

I'm almost used to the constant ache. I unwrap the bandage and show Jack.

'They did it to everyone at the feedstore. All the kids.'

Jack is furious.

We dig for an hour hardly saying a word. Finally, Jack is standing thigh deep in the grave. He throws his shovel onto the pile of dirt and says, 'That'll do. It's only gotta be deep enough to keep the foxes out.'

Steb and Simmo appear over by the shearing shed. They pull the plastic off the bodies and drag them, one at a time, to the grave. There are seven. I do the maths in my head: twenty came from Longley, plus the two prisoners who were already here, Steb and Jack killed half a dozen before they even got into the valley and now we're burying seven. That means at least nine have taken off. If they join forces with Tusker, or with Ramage, they could still be a problem.

But when I mention this to Jack, he shakes his head. 'The ones that escaped won't be in any hurry to come back here,' he says.

The four of us fill the grave over the slumped corpses. My arm is throbbing now, but I enjoy the short walk back down to the sheds with the men. I feel like I'm part of something, one of them.

Steb and Simmo wander off but Jack hangs back. When they're gone he asks me what happened with Ramage yesterday.

I do my best to explain—it feels like I'm unloading a burden.

Jack leans against the shed wall, his face turned to the sun, hands in his pockets. 'How do you feel about it, now?' he says.

'I dunno. Half the time I think I should've killed him, the other half I think I did the right thing.'

'I guess we'll know soon enough.' He can't hide the disappointment in his voice.

As the days pass, Harry improves only to slip back into unconsciousness again. Kas and I take our turn at sitting with him during the night. Stella is directing all her attention to Hope, feeding and changing her, playing with her, rocking her to sleep. I'm sure Kas feels she should be taking more responsibility, but she knows Stella is better equipped to do it—and it gives her a distraction from what's happening with Harry.

Each night, Kas treats the wound on my arm, gently rubbing cream into the burn. The redness is retreating but that just highlights the 'R' more. I hate looking at it. I hate what Ramage thinks it means. I touch the raised skin on the back of Kas's hand.

'Now you know what it feels like,' she says.

The farmers are three men down without Harry, Vic and Will, and there's a lot of work to be done in the paddocks. The fighting has delayed the spring planting so our days are spent walking behind a bullock-drawn plough, dropping seeds into the dark soil.

I look across at Kas as she walks along the other side of a furrow. The wind blows her hair in wisps over her face. She tucks it behind her ear, looks up and smiles.

'What?' she says.

'Just looking,' I say, returning her smile.

But we soon fall back into the work again. The same thought is playing on both of us. *What happens next?* Kas hasn't said anything more about staying but, as things start to settle in the valley and the days get longer, my mind is turning to the coast.

A week passes and we think we've lost Harry half a dozen times, but he keeps fighting back. He's like a drowning man, just making it to the surface for a gulp of air before sinking again. Somehow, he keeps finding the surface just in time. He's not as feverish as he was but the wound isn't healing and most mornings the sheets are stained with blood.

Finally, he stays conscious long enough to talk. His voice is dry and Stella spoons soup and water into his mouth. She has to put her ear close to his lips to hear what he's saying. It doesn't make much sense but I see the relief on Stella's face with him trying to communicate.

We're a month into spring. The wildflowers are creeping out of the bush into the paddocks, and the flies have returned to pester us. I help Jack reinforce the fences, while Kas moves cattle down onto the river flats, happy to be back riding Yogi. Rowdy follows me everywhere, worried I might go off and leave him again. He's moving much more freely, though he favours one leg.

Stella is returning to her old self. She can see Harry getting a little stronger every day and she's like a proud mum with Hope. Every morning she's up before the rest of us, seeing that she is fed and happy. When the time comes to head out to the paddocks, Stella fits her into the papoose and does her fair share of the planting. Kas watches this each morning and I get the sense she's weighing up what's best for Hope against the promise she made to Rose. We haven't spoken about leaving yet but the time is coming. Most of the planting is done and, even though we're welcome to stay in the community, the coast is calling me. I want Kas to come with me, but I'm nervous about bringing it up. We're treated as adults here, included in all the decision-making, and I notice the affect this has on Kas. It's like she has a new sense of herself. She smiles more easily and dags around like an idiot when there's just the two of us. She doesn't tense up when Stella hugs her and she's like a big sister to Willow.

After dinner one night we walk up to the rocky outcrop above the home paddock. We climb to the top and look down at the farmhouses and sheds. Kas sits with her knees drawn up to her chest.

'It's so beautiful here,' she says.

I sit next to her. The sun has dropped behind the ridge and it shoots golden rays through the treetops. There's no wind and the crickets are making a racket in the still air.

'I don't know what to do, Finn,' she says. 'I want to stay and help raise Hope, but I don't want to lose you.'

She sweeps her hair behind her ear, revealing the birthmark on her face.

'You remember the argument we had up here?' she says. 'When we first arrived with Willow.'

'Yeah. You said I should make decisions with my head and not my heart.'

'I was wrong,' she says. 'It's not always one or the other, is it? Sometimes it's both.'

'I don't know what to say, Kas.'

She turns to me. 'Stella is a better mother than I'll ever be. If we stayed, I'm not even sure what use I'd be. But I promised Rose.'

Thoughts are flying through my head: about Angowrie, about Mum and Dad, about where I belong. But, above all that, there's this ache to be with Kas.

'I made that promise, too. And I want to be with you, regardless.' I can hardly believe I'm saying the words aloud.

She smiles, then, and gives the smallest shake of her head.

I have to look away. I could stay here but it would never be home. Not without the salt in the air and the constant sound of the ocean as a backdrop to everything.

Kas places her hands on either side of my face and turns me to her. She brings her mouth close enough for me to feel her breath on my lips.

'I'm coming with you to the coast,' she says. She's smiling and crying and it's like something lets go inside me, something that's been caged up forever and now it's free.

Three weeks after Harry was shot, he's able to sit up in bed and feed himself. He struggles with it but he's determined to get some strength back into his body. He's frustrated at not being able to work alongside the others but it will be a while before he's fit enough to do that. Each evening I come into his room and give him a report on the work we've done that day—the ploughing, the sowing, the digging out of thistles and the fencing. He makes suggestions about what else needs to be done.

Tonight, after I've given him my report, he stops and looks long and hard at me. 'What are your plans, Finn?' he asks.

We've been delaying the decision to leave. It's hard work here but there's something comforting in the routine and in helping out on the farm. And there's the company of people, too. When we return to Angowrie there'll just be Kas and me, at least until JT, Daymu and the others arrive—though there's no guarantee the No-landers will let them go.

'We're going back to the coast,' I say. 'When the sowing's done here and you can get by without us.'

'The work's never done on a farm,' he says, wearily.

'I know, but it's not—'

'Not what?'

'Home.'

He leans back on his pillow and folds his arms. 'And what about Hope?'

'Kas and I think she should stay here. I doubt we'd be able to prise her out of Stella's arms anyway.'

'You're right about that. I told you we lost a child? We both mourned her but I reckon a mother feels it in a deeper way.' He scratches his chin. 'Hope won't bring Holly back but...'

'We'll only be a bit over a day's travel away. We'll come to visit when it's safe.'

'I'm not sure the world's ever going to be safe.'

I tell him about Wentworth, that there's some order being re-established. That there's even electricity.

'That's a long way from here, Finn. And who knows what's happened with the virus. In the meantime, the Wilders are a bigger concern.'

'But the Wilders are scattered. Some of the ones in Longley will've taken their chance and left while Ramage was away.'

'They'll reorganise. It's the way of bastards like that. We'll never be completely safe and neither will you.'

'We saw Tusker up near Swan's Marsh.'

Harry shakes his head. 'Even if you had killed Ramage, Tusker would've taken over.'

'Yeah, I don't think Kas and me are on his Christmas card list, either.'

Harry laughs again, then grabs his side. When he settles he says, 'But, remember, there'll always be a family here for you.'

He puts his hand on my shoulder and pulls me into a hug.

Our preparations to leave are stretched out over the next week. There's not a lot we need to carry with us—travelling light will make the journey easier. More than anything else, we're preparing ourselves for life on our own again. Rowdy is mobile enough to make the trip and Yogi will be coming too—we can use him to carry our gear and the food we'll need. He'll come in handy if we find trouble and need to get away quickly, too. We'll retrace our route via the logging coup and Pinchgut Junction. It'll be tough for Yogi with all the storm damage but Kas is confident she can get him through.

On the night before we leave, a dinner is organised in our honour. Food is pretty scarce and we feel guilty about so much going into one meal but everyone in the community brings something. We're all crowded into Harry and Stella's place. When I look around the room I see the faces of all these people who've become our friends, adults and kids alike. The only ones missing are Vic and Will. It's been weeks now and there's still no sign of them.

We are about to start eating when Harry calls from the bedroom.

Stella and I walk into the room and find him sitting up on the side of the bed, his big feet planted on the floor and an old dressing gown pulled around his frame.

'You weren't gonna start without me, were you?' he says.

Stella and I help him up and shuffle him out into the kitchen.

'Excellent,' Jack says when he sees Harry. 'We need a scarecrow for the corn field.'

'Yeah. Stuff you too, Jack!' Harry says.

We eat dried meat, potatoes and greens and it feels like a feast. Before we start, Stella brings us all into a circle around the table and we link arms. I have Kas on one side and Willow on the other, her arm pulling me in close to her.

'Lord,' Stella says, the room hushed. 'Bless our little community and the food we share tonight. And bless these two,' she nods at Kas and me. 'We love them and we ask that you look over them and keep them safe. Amen.' Kas turns her head and presses her forehead to my shoulder.

No one wants to leave after the meal is finished. They crowd around Harry, joking with him and talking farming. But he tires quickly and Stella and Jack are soon helping him back to his room. Finally everyone drifts off to their own houses, leaving Kas and me with Stella, Willow and Hope, who is bright-eyed with all the noise and conversation. Willow has hardly let go of my good arm, tugging me to ask all sorts of questions about rabbit trapping, crayfish and abalone diving. She makes me promise that when she's a bit older, we'll take her down to the coast for a summer.

Later, Kas and I sit outside. 'We should sleep,' I say. 'We've got a long day of travelling tomorrow.'

She doesn't say anything for a while. I've almost drifted off when she says, 'I've never had anything like this before. It's strange.' She turns to face me. 'We're just gonna have each other down on the coast.' She laces her fingers through mine. 'Are you okay with that?'

'Only for fifty years, or so,' I say trying not to smile.

'You mean until I've got wrinkles and saggy boobs?'

'Yeah, and I've got grey hair and tuck-shop arms.'

She laughs and I put my arms around her and hold her tight.

The whole community gathers in the yard to see us off. It's a clear, crisp morning, without a cloud in the sky. The sun has yet to top the ridge and a mist hovers over the paddocks. Yogi is saddled and laden with our gear. Rowdy hops around like a mad dog, eager to get going.

We say our goodbyes, and Rachel hugs both of us. Jack shakes my hand the firmest, and James and Kate mumble their farewells. Harry has made his way out onto the porch and leans on one of the posts. He's trying to keep his emotions in check but his voice wavers when he speaks. 'You look after each other, now,' he says.

Willow can't bring herself to look at us. Stella has Hope on her hip. She passes her to Kas, who lifts her up and kisses her. 'I'll see you soon,' she says. Slowly, reluctantly, she passes her to me.

Looking at her little face, I see so much of Rose looking back at me. Her hand curls around my finger. I kiss her on the forehead and give her back to Stella.

Finally, Willow throws herself at me, almost knocking me over. 'Bye, Finn,' she says, her bottom lip quivering. 'You're my brother, now.'

'And you're my sister.'

She nods her head and steps towards Kas, who struggles to pick her up. 'You're getting too big for this,' Kas says.

'Make sure you come back and see me,' Willow says.

Stella walks the first few metres with us, carrying Hope. She stops when we reach the gate into the top paddock and draws us both to her. 'Willow's right,' she says. 'You're family, now. There will always be a home for you here.'

She kisses both of us on the cheek and swipes a tear away. 'Go now,' she says. 'Travel safe.'

Kas leads Yogi through the gate and I follow with Rowdy.

When we reach the top fence we stop and look back down to the house. Everyone else has headed off to work but two figures stand in the yard, waving—Harry and Stella, supporting each other. Willow balances on a fencepost, her arms waving wildly and her mess of blonde curls flying in the wind.

25

The journey home takes longer than we expect. Wherever our path is blocked by a fallen tree or branch we have to find a way of getting Yogi around it. Rowdy slows us down too. His wounds have healed but he's lost a lot of condition. He struggles to walk for more than an hour without a rest.

We spend a night in the bush just short of Pinchgut Junction. We get a fire going, and feed it through the night. There are still some glowing coals in the morning. By this stage we figure the hardest part of the trip is behind us, the rugged country along the ridge and the climb up the rock face with Yogi. He handled it better this time, but it was pretty sketchy for a while, not that Kas would let on. She reckons it was easier the second time round.

By late afternoon on the second day we get our first glimpse of the coast, a line of deep blue on the horizon. The wind pushes the salt air up to meet us and I stop and fill my lungs with the smell of home. It reaches out to me, pulling me the last few kilometres. Kas senses it too. She's stripped down to a singlet and shorts in the warm afternoon and sweat beads on her skin. She leads Yogi by the reins and smiles at me, shaking her head.

'I see you, dog boy,' she says, 'sniffing the wind and walking quicker.'

'Don't tell me you don't feel it, too?'

'Not like you—I'm a farm girl, remember. I can barely swim.'

'We'll fix that over summer.'

'You just want to see me in my undies,' she laughs.

'Never even thought about that.'

We've been pretty casual about the journey up until now, confident that no one would have been made their way through to the coast while we've been gone. But as we get closer to Angowrie, we turn off the road so we can follow the bush tracks. We pass the ruins of the hayshed and the fence where I've trapped rabbits for the last three years. Finally, we reach the top of the ridge with a view over town. From up here it looks unchanged, the houses sitting down among the tea trees and moonah, the burnt-out shops along the main street and the big Shell petrol station sign standing above it all. I follow the river to its mouth where the even, breaking lines tell me the surf's up.

There's no sign of life, no movement, no smoke, no noise—Angowrie looks just like it did when we left—dead, yet somehow alive.

We walk cautiously down the hill to the bridge. As we get lower I hear the breaking waves echoing up the valley, a sound that brings a smile to my face. Rowdy pads along without a care in the world, happy to be in familiar surroundings. He pisses on every tree and gatepost, until he can't have a drop left in him. We scout the bridge before crossing and quickly move up into the cover of the houses along the main road. I could navigate blindfolded from here. When we reach the driveway of the house in front of ours, we tie Yogi to a tree and follow the line of sheoaks to the back shed. From there, we get a clear view of the house.

Straightaway I know there's something wrong. Before we left we trashed the place to make it look like no one had been living here. We left the backdoor hanging by a single hinge and broke some windows. The door's been rehung and plywood covers the broken windows. And there's a wisp of smoke coming out of the chimney.

Before I can grab him, Rowdy is at the door and inside. We hear the scraping of a chair on the floor and the door closes. I slide the rifle off my shoulder and check the bolt.

'That you, Finn?'

I can't believe what I'm hearing but the voice is unmistakable.

Ray steps out onto the porch and leans against the rail. 'Took your bloody time,' he says, a smile breaking across his weathered face.

'Yeah,' I say, trying to keep the excitement out of my voice, 'we've been a bit busy.'

I walk across the yard and he makes his way down the steps. I'm careful not to bowl him over but I hug him long and hard. 'Shit, Ray, we thought you were dead.'

'I feel like I am some mornings.'

Kas stands beside us. I have to remind myself they hardly know each other—there were just the two days at Ray's place when Hope was born. Still, he reaches out, pulls her to him and kisses her forehead. 'Thought I'd lost you two,' he says. 'Come inside.'

I never noticed the smell of my place before, I was so used to it. Now though, there's the musty odour of damp furniture and wood smoke. It looks clean. Ray's been here for a while.

'I like what you've done with the place,' I say.

'Yeah, must have been a rough mob here before me. Left it looking like a pigsty,' he says, his face giving nothing away.

Kas struggles to understand this sort of conversation, the dry humour of it. She looks at one of us, then the other, shaking her head. 'I never know when you're being serious,' she says.

'It's bloke talk,' Ray says. 'All bullshit.'

He motions us to sit down as he stokes the firebox in the stove and puts the kettle on the hotplate. 'I've been making tea from dried dandelion flowers. It tastes like cat's piss but I'm getting used to it. I'll make you a cuppa.'

I'm still blown away that Ray's alive. I'm so happy to see him but I want to know how he got here.

'We went to your place, Ray. It was burnt to the ground.

What happened out there?' I ask.

'Fuckers,' he says, 'excuse my French.' He sighs and sits down opposite us at the table. 'At the start of winter, three Wilders turned up. They were hunting for you two but when the storms hit they turfed me out into the shed and took over the house.'

'Three?' Kas says.

'Yeah, why?' Ray asks.

'We met them when we went out to see you near the end of the winter,' she says. 'There were only two.'

Ray looks past us to the stove.

'They chased me off,' he says. 'Chased me off my own land, the bastards. But I killed one of them. Didn't mean too. Got angry, that's all.'

'So they burned your house down,' I say.

'I don't even know if they meant to. Thick as bricks, the other two. I reckon they knocked a lamp over.'

He looks straight at us then, his head turned slightly to the side, questioning. 'What happened when you found them there?'

I look to Kas but her head is down and she runs a finger along the wood grain on the tabletop. 'They won't be bothering anyone again,' I say, with a quick shake of my head so Ray doesn't keep asking.

He nods and gets to his feet. The kettle has boiled. He makes the tea and pours three cups. I take a sip. 'You're right,' I say. 'Cat's piss.'

We talk until the light falls away, telling Ray everything that's happened since we left Angowrie. He smiles when he hears about Hope, and fumes when I show him the branding on my arm. 'Treating people like animals! What's the world come to?' he says.

Eventually, our stomachs remind us we've hardly eaten all day. Ray's been tending my veggie patch in the house up the street and he's discovered the chooks' nest under the cypress trees.

'Wasn't hard to find where you hid the key to the stores,' he says. 'I haven't used much but I had to change the gas bottle last week.'

We feast on eggs, fried beans and baked potatoes. More than anything else, the meal brings me back home. I ate like this for two winters on my own and now here I am, back again and sharing food with Kas and Ray. Rowdy wolfs down a can of sausages in about ten seconds.

With full bellies, our minds turn to survival again.

Ray winks at me. 'I reckon there'd be a heap of rabbits up in the farmland. I'd kill for a nice tender bunny cooked up with a few veggies.'

'Abalone first!' Kas says. 'I want abalone.'

'Crayfish. Mussels. Flathead,' I say.

It seems like everything is possible again, that we'll be able to do more than just survive. We're pretty sure we're safe, for the time being at least—we might even make it through the summer without having to worry about Wilders. And each day we'll keep an eye out for JT and Daymu.

After Ray has gone to bed, I take Kas out through the sheoaks at the back of the block. I don't need a torch. I know every twist and turn in the track to the beach. I can just make out Rowdy ahead of us. He doesn't turn to look; he knows where we're going. Kas slides her hand behind my back and we walk arm in arm.

We climb the steps to the platform as the moon rises out of the sea to the east. It spreads a pale yellow shimmer across the surface that looks like a path laid just for us. The glow catches the whitewater as the waves break along the sandbar to the river mouth. There's barely any wind and the air is still warm. Now Kas pulls me along by my hand, down the dune to the open beach. When we get there she stops in front of me and smiles. She peels the jumper and singlet over her head and drops her shorts to the sand.

'Come on, then,' she says. 'I might drown on my own.' She turns and runs towards the water.

I strip as quickly as I can and peel the bandage off my arm. She's stopped at the edge, the waves touching her feet. 'So cold!' she yells, but I knock her off balance and she staggers into the water. The waves knock us off our feet again and again but we bob back up and hurl ourselves at them. Kas is squealing and laughing and so am I. Rowdy paces up and down on the sand, barking and snapping at the white water.

The salt stings the burn on my arm but I know it'll help it heal.

Finally, we stagger back into the shallows. Kas is just ahead of me when she turns and opens her arms. Her body shines in the moonlight, glistening wet. I fall into her and I don't think any force, no matter how strong, could pull us apart. She kisses me and I never want her to stop.

We take our time to walk up the beach, me turning to follow each wave as it breaks on the bar. 'I think I'll have a surf in the morning, first thing,' I say.

'No you won't,' she says.

'I won't?'

'No. Tomorrow morning you're giving me my first surfing lesson.'

We dress quickly and climb the dune back to the platform, the same dune Rose and me ran up to escape Ramage that first day. I can't even begin to think how long ago that was or how much my life has changed since. She brought danger with her but now, with Kas's hand warm in mine, I'm glad she arrived. I'm glad I helped her. I wish she was here with us, but somehow part of her always will be.

We stop for a while on the platform, me looking to the ocean and Kas gazing back towards town.

'*Finn!*' she says suddenly.

'What?' I look around but all I see is the vague outline of the main road, the shadows of houses and ruined buildings—everything as it's been for three years.

'Wait,' she says, both hands locked around my arm. 'Look.'

All over town the streetlights flicker for an instant, hold their glow, then die.

ACKNOWLEDGMENTS

This book was written with the support of a number of organisations and individuals. Thanks to Margaret River Press for the use of their beautiful house and studio; to the National Writers House, Varuna; and to Jason, Anna, Matilda and Harriet for the use of my writing home-away-from-home at Falmouth (again…and again).

Thanks to my coastal support team led by Nicole Maher and Great Escape Books—and to both Nic and Kai for their reading of the early drafts. Your enthusiasm and advocacy for my books has been nothing short of amazing.

Thanks to my fellow writers who have been sounding boards and partners in crime: Jock Serong, and the 'Class of

2016', Melanie Cheng, Kate Mildenhall, Rajith Savanadasa and Michelle Wright.

Thanks to all the crew at Text, especially Jane Pearson, editor extraordinaire, Nadja Poljo, the best publicist a writer could wish for, and Shalini Kunahlan for her inspired marketing ideas.

Thanks to St Bernard's College and the staff at Santa Monica for supporting my work and to the hundreds of boys over the years who unwittingly provided the insights that led to the creation of Finn.

Thanks to Oliver, Maddy and Harley for their love and support, and for reminding me there are sometimes more important things in the world than writing a book—like bluebird days at Vail.

And finally, and most importantly, thanks to Lynne, who has done more than anyone to support my writing. None of this would have been possible without your love and understanding.